Praise for Kit Pearson

PUFFIN CANADA

A HANDFUL OF TIME

KIT PEARSON was born in Edmonton and grew up there and in Vancouver. Her previous seven novels (six of which have been published by Penguin) have been published in Canada, in English and French, and in the United States, Australia, New Zealand, Japan, the Netherlands, Germany, Great Britain, China, and Korea. She has received fourteen awards for her writing, including the Vicky Metcalf Award for her body of work. She presently lives in Victoria.

Visit her website: www.kitpearson.com.

Also by Kit Pearson

The Daring Game

The Sky Is Falling

Looking at the Moon

The Lights Go On Again

Awake and Dreaming

This Land: An Anthology of Canadian Stories
for Young Readers
(as editor)

Whispers of War:
The War of 1812 Diary of Susanna Merritt

A Perfect Gentle Knight

A Handful
of Time

KIT PEARSON

PUFFIN
CANADA

PUFFIN CANADA

Published by the Penguin Group

Penguin Group (Canada), 90 Eglinton Avenue East, Suite 700, Toronto, Ontario, Canada
M4P 2Y3 (a division of Pearson Canada Inc.)

Penguin Group (USA) Inc., 375 Hudson Street, New York, New York 10014, U.S.A.
Penguin Books Ltd, 80 Strand, London WC2R 0RL, England
Penguin Ireland, 25 St Stephen's Green, Dublin 2, Ireland(a division of Penguin Books Ltd)
Penguin Group (Australia), 250 Camberwell Road, Camberwell, Victoria 3124, Australia
(a division of Pearson Australia Group Pty Ltd)
Penguin Books India Pvt Ltd, 11 Community Centre, Panchsheel Park, New Delhi – 110 017, India
Penguin Group (NZ), 67 Apollo Drive, Rosedale, North Shore 0632, Auckland, New Zealand
(a division of Pearson New Zealand Ltd)
Penguin Books (South Africa) (Pty) Ltd, 24 Sturdee Avenue, Rosebank, Johannesburg 2196,
South Africa

Penguin Books Ltd, Registered Offices: 80 Strand, London WC2R 0RL, England

First published in Viking Kestrel by Penguin Group (Canada),
a division of Pearson Canada Inc., 1987
Published in Puffin Canada paperback by Penguin Group (Canada),
a division of Pearson Canada Inc., 1988
Published in this edition, 2007

1 2 3 4 5 6 7 8 9 10 (OPM)

ISBN-13: 978-0-14-305638-6
ISBN-10: 0-14-305638-7

Library and Archives Canada Cataloguing in Publication data available upon request.

Visit the Penguin Group (Canada) website at **www.penguin.ca**

Special and corporate bulk purchase rates available; please see
www.penguin.ca/corporatesales or call 1-800-810-3104, ext. 477 or 474

In memory of my aunt
Mollie Mackenzie

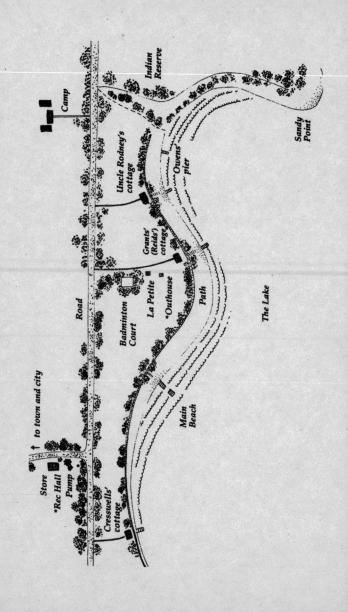

Camp

Indian
Reserve

Uncle Rodney's
cottage

Owens
pier

Sandy
Point

Grants'
(Reids')
cottage

Road

*Outhouse

Badminton
Court

La Petite

Path

The Lake

← to town and city

Store
*Rec Hall
Pump

Cresswells'
cottage

Main
Beach

"You might say," Tom said slowly,… "You might say that different people have different times, although of course, they're really all bits of the same big Time."

PHILLIPPA PEARCE
TOM'S MIDNIGHT GARDEN

1

*P*atricia knew she had made a mistake as soon as she got the canoe into the water. The long, green boat had looked so solid on the beach, but once afloat, it seemed to come alive. Patricia had to wade after it quickly before it nosed away. At least she'd remembered to put in the paddle. She swung her leg over one tippy side and gave a sort of jump into its safe middle.

But it wasn't safe at all. The paddle kept sliding down in her hands. She couldn't duplicate her cousin Kelly's smooth strokes; hers were short and splashy and made the canoe travel in a jerky circle.

Patricia felt more and more hot and nervous as she realized she couldn't bring the boat back to shore. She dreaded having to call for help. Kelly would come running down the steps and make fun of her Eastern cousin for being so inept.

Just then a spurt of wind blew the canoe farther out. In desperation Patricia stood up and tried to pole her way in, but the paddle stuck in the lake bottom. Trying to hang onto it, she leaned forward as far as she could—and fell into the lake.

HALF AN HOUR LATER she sat, changed but still shivering, on the edge of Kelly's bed. Her wet clothes lay in a sodden pile at her feet. She was afraid to open the door as she listened to the low voices coming from the other side of it.

"I'm telling you, Mum, this is the last straw! If Mr. Donaldson hadn't been there, the canoe would have drifted all the way down the lake. And she lost the paddle, too. I had to swim out and get it. She's hopeless!"

"Kelly!" Aunt Ginnie's voice was quiet but sharp. "I won't have you talking about Patricia like this. It wasn't her fault—she doesn't know about boats."

"That's the whole point! Why did she do it, then?"

"Shush! She'll hear you. She probably wanted to prove herself. None of you has given her much of a welcome so far. Why wasn't she with you all at Uncle Rod's?"

"Oh, well …" Kelly paused. "She must have sneaked away or something, I don't know. But does she have to be with us every minute of the day?"

Through her misery Patricia felt a twinge of anger. Kelly was lying. She and her brother and sister had run off before Patricia could see where they were going.

"Kelly," said Aunt Ginnie firmly, "I'm very disappointed in you. Patricia is our guest for two months. She isn't used to a lot of children, or to a cottage and a lake. You must be nice to her. Especially because …"

Don't tell her! prayed Patricia, digging her nails into her palms. Uncle Doug had promised not to.

"Because why?"

"Because she's my sister's only child and she's away from home and I want her to be happy here. So you and Trevor and the others have to help her feel at home. Especially you, because you're the oldest. Do you understand? If I hear you're neglecting her again, I'm going to be very angry."

"Oh, all right," Kelly said darkly.

Patricia sighed. If Aunt Ginnie got mad at Kelly, her cousin would just take it out all the more on her.

She had to open the door. They must be wondering what she was doing in there for so long. As she ventured into the living room the two figures turned quickly.

Aunt Ginnie smiled—a pleasant smile that dimpled her round cheeks. But as usual Patricia avoided looking too closely into the friendly face.

"There you are, Patricia dear. All dry? Not cold, I hope. At least no harm was done, and I have an idea. When you feel you're ready, how about Kelly giving you some lessons? Canoeing isn't hard to learn." She put her arm around her niece, who didn't answer but looked nervously at Kelly.

"Let's go back to Uncle Rod's," her cousin muttered. "They're all waiting for me."

Patricia followed Kelly's angry back out of the cottage. The very worst thing she could imagine right now was being in that tippy canoe with Kelly.

*O*nly the morning before, Patricia had been standing in the Toronto airport, trying to say goodbye to her mother. They stared at each other self-consciously.

Her mother kept checking her watch while she twitched at the skirt of her daughter's new dress. "Stand up straight, darling. You always look so bunchy. Now, try to control how much you eat this summer. Look at people when they talk to you and don't mumble. And have a wonderful time. Your—your father and I will miss you." Then she smiled. "Who's going to cook for me? I'll have to go out for every meal! I'm sorry I can't wait to see you onto the plane, but I'm already late."

Her briefcase poking into Patricia's side, she kissed her daughter briskly and hurried away.

The passenger agent standing beside Patricia—her name was Debra and she smelled of deodorant—beamed with approval. "Your mother's so attractive. Haven't I seen her somewhere before?"

"She's the host of 'CBC Newswatch,'" mumbled Patricia.

"Of course—Ruth Reid! I watch her program all the time. And your father's Harris Potter the journalist. I read that article about them in last month's *Toronto Life*. Your Mum sure looks young for forty-seven."

Patricia hung her head. She often wished she could be invisible. She didn't like being in the spotlight of her parents' prominence.

"There was a picture of *you* in that magazine, too, I remember," said Debra as they made their way to Gate 74 to board the plane.

Patricia hated the picture. In it, the three of them were sitting on the steps of their renovated Cabbagetown home. Her parents looked handsome; Patricia looked as plain as ever, her face hidden under her stringy bangs. Still, she could remember a moment of unusual security, squeezed between her mother and father, each with an arm around her. In the magazine they looked like a happy, united family.

But the photograph was a fraud. Debra would react differently if she knew Patricia was being sent West for the summer while her parents worked out the details of their separation.

ON THE PLANE a chatty older couple plied her with uncomfortable questions. How old was she? How did she like school? Why was she going to Edmonton?

Patricia answered as shortly as possible but she spoke so softly they kept asking her to repeat herself. She could tell they thought she looked young for twelve. The flight attendant, too, kept disturbing her with fussy instructions.

She poked at her lunch in its plastic container and sighed. A small overdone steak, mushy green beans and a tired salad. Munching slowly on the roll, she made up another menu. Quiche would be perfect for a plane, maybe with spinach and Swiss cheese. And green beans could be marinated, the way she had tried doing them last week.

When she had gone through several possible menus, she began to think about her relatives instead of food. She had never met Aunt Ginnie and Uncle Doug and their four children; her mother had such a full timetable that the two families had always put off getting together. Every Christmas Patricia examined the photographs of her cousins curiously. They all looked so self-assured, she knew she wouldn't know what to say to them.

At least there was a baby. Maybe she could help take care of it. Once she had asked her parents if they would have another child.

"Not at my age, darling," her mother had laughed. "I was almost too old when I had *you*! No more babies for me."

AT THE AIRPORT in Edmonton Patricia waited with another passenger agent until a small, wiry man in Bermuda shorts hurried up to them. He had thick pepper-and-salt hair and a mild expression behind his glasses. "Patricia? Patricia Potter? I'm your Uncle Doug."

He picked up Patricia's suitcase and led her out to the car. "We're going straight to the lake," he informed her. "It's not far—about eighty kilometres out of the city."

He spoke of "the lake" as if there were no other. So had Patricia's mother. "Your aunt and uncle have invited you to the lake this summer," she had told her daughter towards the end of school.

Patricia had shivered, picturing a huge expanse of water covering Western Canada like a small sea. "Is there only one lake in Alberta?" she asked timidly.

Her mother sighed impatiently. "Of course not, darling. It's just an expression, like people in Ontario talk about 'the cottage.'"

"In Vermont they say 'the camp,'" put in her father, who had grown up in New England. He told Patricia the name of the lake and showed her in an atlas how small it was.

Patricia had tried to get her mother to describe it more, but even though she'd spent all her childhood summers at the lake, she was vague. "I don't remember much about it and it's probably changed a lot anyhow. But don't worry about it, darling. You'll have a marvellous time with cousins your own age to play with."

Uncle Doug was asking her a few questions about her flight and the weather in Toronto, but he didn't seem to mind when Patricia barely answered. She was grateful when he switched on the car radio.

Brown, green and bright yellow fields flashed by. Over the hilly countryside arched an enormous sky. It made Patricia feel small and unimportant. Her dress was wrinkled and damp from the hours of sitting on the plane and her hair stuck to the back of her neck.

Uncle Doug turned off the music. "Your aunt asked me to talk to you about something, Patricia," he began hesitantly. "We haven't told our children or anyone else about your parents. If you want to discuss it with us we'll want to listen, but we won't bring it up unless you do. When it becomes public at the end of the summer you and Aunt Ginnie can decide what to say. For now we're going to forget about it. We want you to relax and have a good time for the next couple of months, all right?"

Patricia wished she could forget about it. She felt a dangerous wetness in her eyes at his kind words. Her uncle's awkwardness reminded her of her father's goodbye last night.

"I'll miss you very much, Patricia," he had murmured, sitting by her bed. "I thought you and I could find out how to make sushi this summer. This will all work out for the best, though." He sounded unconvinced, but he took her hand and carried on. "You know that, no matter what, I'll always be your father and I'll still ... I'll still love you."

Patricia squirmed with embarrassment for both of them. Her father was not a person who talked easily about feelings. In fact, he rarely talked at all. He seemed more comfortable with his word processor or his Cuisinart than with people.

Patricia believed what he said, though. The two of them had always had a silent regard for each other. But he sounded as if he were talking in a book, like the one her mother had just bought for her—*The Boys' and Girls' Book about Divorce*. After she had kissed her father goodbye, she pulled the blankets tightly around her, even though it was a hot night ...

Now her uncle's car was pulling off the highway onto a bumpy road. "There's the lake!" said Uncle Doug. He seemed relieved to change the subject. "My brood always competes to see who can spot it first."

Patricia glimpsed a band of blue between two hills. Then they lost sight of it as the road curved past a log building labelled Store and swung left past a series of driveways, each marked with a name painted on a board.

When they turned in at the sign that said Grant, Patricia began to twist the material of her dress in her damp hands. A black dog that looked like a wolf pelted towards them and barked hysterically, leaping up to the car as it inched down the long driveway.

"That's Peggy," laughed Uncle Doug. Patricia slumped farther into her seat each time the dog's head appeared at the window.

They stopped at the back of a shabby-looking green cottage. It seemed as if hundreds of people were pouring out of it and running towards the car with cries of welcome, but when Patricia counted, there were really only five.

She stiffened at her aunt's embrace. The baby was part of the hug and grinned toothlessly at her.

"Patricia, we're so glad you're here! Let me take a look at you. You're not like Ruth, are you?"

Patricia was used to being told she didn't look like her beautiful mother. Now she realized that she took after her aunt—short and plump.

Aunt Ginnie gave her niece a searching, sympathetic look. Patricia averted her eyes and dropped her head as her cousins were introduced.

Kelly was the oldest. She had the kind of assured good looks that the popular girls at school had—tall, fair and slender. Trevor was stocky, with a sunburnt nose. Skinny Maggie stuck her tongue out. The cheerful baby was Rosemary.

"You're just in time for lunch!" bubbled Aunt Ginnie. Slowly, Patricia began to feel a bit more cheerful.

They ate on the sloping front lawn of the Grants' cottage. It was high above the lake, which stretched out below as far as Patricia could see, the towering sky extending its blueness. The grass prickled her legs uncomfortably as she gulped down a chicken salad sandwich. Kelly and Trevor stared at her when she took two more.

They think I'm greedy, she thought, but she was too hungry to care. At least the food was going to be good.

Uncle Doug came over to her and pointed out landmarks.

"That ugly tower far to the right is a power plant. We all hate it—it makes the water too weedy and spoils the view. And all that green to the left is an Indian Reserve."

Patricia nodded politely but didn't reply. It was just as it had been on the plane—the more people tried to draw her out, the more she wanted to disappear.

The only unthreatening person in the family was the baby, who lolled on a blanket beside her and crowed with joy. Patricia stuck a tentative finger in her fist and Rosemary gripped it with surprising strength.

"She's the easiest baby I've had," said Aunt Ginnie. "Always in a good mood. I think she finds us all very amusing."

Then her aunt took Rosemary in for a nap and Uncle Doug followed them. Maggie had wandered off. Now Patricia had to face her older cousins alone. She clutched her knees to her chest and pretended to be looking at the view.

"No one wears skirts at the lake," Kelly said flatly, stretching out the long tanned legs that emerged from her ragged cut-off jeans.

"I came here straight from the plane, that's why I'm dressed up," mumbled Patricia. "I have shorts in my suit-case."

"How old are you?" Kelly asked her.

"Twelve."

"Twelve! Are you sure? Mum said you were my age."

"I turned twelve in May," said Patricia, suddenly feeling as if she weren't actually sure.

"You don't *look* older than me," said Kelly doubtfully. She undid a knife she had strapped to her belt and began whittling on a twig.

"How come you're staying for the whole summer?" asked Trevor. He made it sound like an eternity.

Patricia tugged some clover out of the lawn. "My parents both have a lot of work to do. They wanted me out of the way." That, at least, was the truth.

"We've seen your mother on TV and Mum showed us your dad's column. What's it like having such famous parents? Have you ever been to the TV studio? Did you like being in that article your mum sent?" Kelly seemed really curious and her voice was friendly for the first time.

But Patricia stiffened. "I'd rather not talk about that stuff," she said abruptly.

"You don't have to be snobby about it," said Kelly. She turned to her brother and nodded.

"I guess we'll give you our present now, Patricia," announced Trevor. His round freckled face grinned as he pulled a small blue box out of his pocket and handed it over.

Patricia took it warily. She lifted the lid, then squealed as a tiny brown toad dropped into her lap.

"It's just a toad—are you afraid of it?" Trevor captured the toad and held it close to her face. "Here, take it."

This was a test Patricia knew she would fail. She just couldn't touch the dry, throbbing skin. "N-no thanks," she mumbled, getting up. "Where can I go and change?"

Kelly shrugged, looking disappointed. "Mum'll tell you," she said, dismissing her.

For the rest of that first day Patricia's cousins ignored her and she tried to stay away from the advances of her well-meaning aunt and uncle. As she wolfed down the comforting dinner, she was tempted to tell Aunt Ginnie about her own recipe for carrot cake. But then she'd have to speak; it was safer to remain silent.

The end of the day was the worst. She had to share a bed with Kelly. She had never slept in the same bed, or even in the same room, as anyone else. Patricia lay stiffly on the inside edge, as far away from Kelly as she could get. "I hope you don't kick," was all her cousin said.

The wind in the trees sounded like rain. Patricia shivered and drew the flannelette sheets and heavy satin quilt closer around her neck. She didn't get to sleep for a long time.

3

*T*he second day, the one that ended so disastrously with the canoe, began with meeting even more cousins—Christie and Bruce Reid, whose cottage was four doors away. Both had narrow faces and wavy red hair, Christie's falling down her back and caught at the sides with barrettes shaped like horses. She was ten and her brother was nine, like Trevor. The two of them eyed Patricia suspiciously, and then squatted with Kelly and Trevor in a corner of the screened verandah as if they were banding against her.

Their parents, Uncle Rod and Aunt Karen, came over with them. They explained that their two older boys were travelling in Europe for the summer. Patricia looked down, away from the curious gaze of all these relatives. Because they were family they seemed to have a special claim on her.

"So this is Ruth's daughter!" said Uncle Rod heartily. He had an almost bald, gleaming head. "Come over here and show me your teeth."

Christie giggled and Patricia flushed a deep red. Why would he want to see her teeth?

"Leave her alone, Rod," objected his tiny wife, who looked much younger than her husband. "Your Uncle Rod's a dentist," she explained. "He can't resist examining people, even when he's supposed to be on holiday."

Patricia clamped her mouth shut and remained sitting on the floor. But Uncle Rod wouldn't leave her alone.

"Do you floss?" he demanded.

Patricia nodded miserably.

"Every day? Nothing like flossing to prevent cavities."

"Rod!" Aunt Ginnie gave her brother a warning look.

It was a relief when Maggie provided a diversion. "*I'll* show you my teeth, Uncle Rod." She opened her mouth wide. "See? I lost two!"

"Did the tooth fairy leave you some money?" asked her uncle.

"Yup." The little girl waited expectantly as Uncle Rod dug in his pockets.

"Here's a supplement."

Maggie examined the quarter he handed her. "The tooth fairy gave me a quarter for *each* tooth," she said firmly.

"Maggie!" Uncle Doug pulled her onto his lap.

"Still trying to get rich, aren't you, Magpie!" chuckled Uncle Rod. "How much money do you have saved up now?"

"I have forty-nine dollars and twenty-one cents in the bank," said Maggie proudly, "and every time I watch Rosemary I get a dime."

"And what will you do with all that money?" asked Aunt Karen.

"I haven't decided yet. But it'll be something very important." Maggie looked smug, perched on her father's knee. Patricia was ashamed to be afraid of a six-year-old, but the little girl's confidence scared her as much as her brother and sister's aloofness.

The older children stood up, and Trevor and Bruce left to go fishing. "Christie and I are going out in the canoe," announced Kelly.

"Take Patricia with you," said her mother. "You do know how to swim, don't you, Patricia?"

When she was satisfied on that point—Patricia took swimming lessons every winter at an indoor pool in Toronto—the three cousins walked down the steep steps that were cut into the bank and led to the lake.

The canoe was pulled onto the pebbly beach. *Loon* was painted on its green side in faded letters.

"Have you ever been in a canoe?" demanded Kelly.

Patricia shook her head. "You can leave me behind if you like. I'll watch you from here."

"Mum said to take you, so you better come. Sit on the floor in the middle and lean against the thwart. And don't move—canoes tip really easily."

Patricia did as she was told. Kelly and Christie pushed out the boat with her in it, then climbed in carefully and began to paddle.

The bottom of the canoe was crossed with wooden ribs that dug into her. It was an odd feeling, sitting so low in the water without actually being in it. Patricia leaned back against the life jacket she was using as a cushion. The sun warmed the top of her head and the canoe bobbed gently. A clean smell, like newly washed clothes, rose from the lake. For the first time since she had come here, she felt calm.

Kelly steered them expertly along the shore. She and Christie began a lively discussion that Patricia couldn't follow. It was something about some kids who lived at the other end of the beach.

"There's the Cresswells' Laser," said Kelly. "What a beauty! They're going in the Sunday race. I hope they lose."

She laid her paddle across the gunwales and gazed at a group of white sails billowing in the distance. Closer to shore, brightly patterned windsurfers fluttered and fell. Kelly sighed. "I wish *we* had a sailboat ... or at least a windsurfer."

"I thought Uncle Doug was going to buy you a second-hand boat this summer," said Christie.

"He was." Kelly tossed her cap of hair angrily. "Then a whole bunch of things happened. Rosemary was born— we didn't predict *her* last summer. Mum was going to go back to teaching so we'd have more money, but now she doesn't want to. And Dad can't take any holidays until August, so there wouldn't be enough time to teach me."

"Never mind, Kelly," said Christie. "At least between us we have two canoes and a rowboat."

There was a long pause. Motorboats droned in the distance and voices shouted instructions to water skiers. The canoe glided almost noiselessly, a small rush of water breaking against its bow. Patricia was grateful that her cousins were paying no attention to her. But then, as if they had secretly agreed to it, they began an interrogation.

"Why haven't you ever been in a canoe, Patricia?" asked Christie.

"I've never been to a lake before," Patricia confessed. "My parents take their holidays in the spring and we go to Bermuda."

"What do you do in the summers, then?" came from Kelly behind her.

"I go to the day-camp that my school runs. They take us to museums and plays and things."

"Museums!" scoffed Kelly. "What a dumb thing to do in the summer!"

"What *can* you do?" asked Christie in her cool little voice. "Can you ride? I win prizes for riding in Edmonton."

"I took riding lessons once, but I didn't like it," said Patricia, shivering at the memory.

"Can you fish? Or make a fire?"

"No." Even though she couldn't see their faces, Patricia felt their disapproval. She forced her voice to be louder. "I can cook, though. My father taught me."

"Cooking!" laughed Christie. "Anyone can cook. I make great rice crispie squares."

Patricia wanted to tell them she could make bread, almost perfect pie crusts and better omelettes than her father. But maybe they'd tease her for having such an old-fashioned interest, the way her mother sometimes did. "Your meals are delicious, darling," she once said, "but I don't want you learning to be a little housewife. Women can do a lot more than cook nowadays."

At lunch Maggie discovered the nickname Patricia had always dreaded. Even after six grades of school she couldn't get used to it.

"Patricia Potter ..." said the little girl slowly. "I know all my letters and both your names start with a P." Then her face lit up. "Pee pee! Pee pee in the potty! Hi, Potty!"

"Maggie, that's enough!" said Aunt Ginnie. "Don't be so rude to Patricia."

But Maggie hissed "Potty" at her several times when her mother wasn't listening.

It was after lunch that her cousins had run away from her on their way to Uncle Rod's. Patricia had wandered down to the beach and found the canoe. It had looked so easy in the morning. Maybe she could teach herself how to paddle and show the others she could do something they could ...

4

*U*ncle Doug left early on Monday to go back to the city for the week. At breakfast, Aunt Ginnie told Patricia that every weekday morning in July the children would be taking swimming lessons at the Main Beach.

"I don't see why," complained Kelly. "It wastes so much time and we all know how to swim."

"You know we'd like you to try for the Red Cross badges," said her mother. "For the rest of the day you can do what you like. If you want to be fed, turn up for meals when I ring the cowbell. Otherwise, you can pack a lunch."

Patricia panicked at the thought of so much free time. In Toronto each moment of her life was carefully arranged so she would be fully occupied until her parents finished work. Every day after school she went to a different activity: swimming, French, piano, gymnastics and debating. Her mother had picked them to encourage Patricia's "physical, creative and social skills." The school she attended, The Learning Place, was also supposed to develop the "whole child."

Patricia didn't care about being "whole." What she liked thinking about, in school and after it, was the menu for the dinner she cooked every night with her father; or, lately, alone, since her father was hardly ever at home anymore.

Aunt Ginnie unbuttoned her blouse and lifted the baby to her breast. Patricia watched, fascinated, as Rosemary sucked noisily with contented whimpers.

"You're a greedy-guts," laughed Aunt Ginnie. "Kelly, why don't you all start down to the Main Beach? I'll follow you as soon as I can."

"We have to stop at Christie and Bruce's first," said Kelly.

"Me too!" cried Maggie.

"No, Mum," Kelly groaned. "Does she always have to tag along?"

"Maggie, you stay and come with me—I'll need your help. Wait for Patricia to finish her cereal, Kelly."

Patricia glanced at Kelly and Trevor. They must think she was as much of a nuisance as Maggie. Taking a deep breath, she asked, "Couldn't I go with *you*, Aunt Ginnie? I could help with the baby."

"Do you really want to?"

Patricia nodded, trying not to notice the glee in her cousin's face. Kelly and Trevor were out of the door like a shot.

A little later, Patricia, feeling self-conscious in just her bathing suit, followed Aunt Ginnie down the narrow path towards the Main Beach. They were loaded down like a caravan. Aunt Ginnie pushed a rattling old baby carriage containing Rosemary, towels, hats, pails, diapers, toys and an umbrella. Patricia carried a picnic basket. Maggie and Peggy led the way, the dog dashing in and out of the bushes with excitement.

It was the first time Patricia had been beyond the Grants' end of the beach. A single line of cottages was set far back from the hilly path. "Cohens, Hills, Rainiers, Cherniaks ..." chanted Maggie. "I know everyone's cottage at the lake."

When they reached a wider part Patricia walked beside her aunt. "How often I've gone along this path!" said Aunt Ginnie contentedly. "Your mother used to have to take me to the Main Beach every day. She must have hated being saddled with her little sister all the time."

Patricia tried to imagine her mother here but all she could think of was how annoyed she would be at getting her shoes dusty on the dirt path.

Aunt Ginnie smiled at her niece. "It's nice of you to help me this morning, Patricia. But you don't have to come with me every day, you know—though I don't blame you for feeling shy with your cousins. They're an unruly group—especially Kelly. And it's hard to make new friends when you're feeling sad. But do you know what the best cure is for being miserable?"

Patricia shook her lowered head, her cheeks burning. She wished Maggie weren't so far ahead; then she could divert Aunt Ginnie from this embarrassing conversation.

"The best thing to do is to stop thinking about yourself and your troubles so much. Try to give your cousins a chance—I'm sure they can help you feel better."

They reached the Main Beach before Patricia had to answer. The carriage was left at the top of the steps while they carried down its contents. Several mothers and a few fathers had already spread themselves and their children over the sand. A huge wet dog jumped up on Patricia while she was being introduced to the group. Just as Uncle Rod had, several people exclaimed, "So this is Ruth's daughter!"

Aunt Ginnie arranged the sleeping baby under the umbrella. Then they watched Maggie and some other young children taking their swimming lesson.

The sun blazed down, making Patricia squint. The water and sky were both the same silvery grey. A wide white pier jutted out into the water. Beyond it was a white raft with a diving board on one end.

Aunt Ginnie rubbed Patricia's back with suntan lotion and Patricia squeezed more onto her arms and legs. She lay on her back, closed her eyes and let the hot sun soothe her. If she could spend all her time with Aunt Ginnie and Rosemary, things would be a lot easier.

But the peace was destroyed by the breathless arrival of Kelly, Trevor, Christie, Bruce and Aunt Karen. Aunt Karen settled down beside Aunt Ginnie and began a nonstop conversation. The others kicked up the sand, ransacked the basket for lemonade and argued about towels. Patricia wondered if they had been talking about her.

When it was time for her swimming lessons she was put in the Grey group, along with the boys and Christie.

They had to swim five lengths back and forth to the raft. Patricia was a fairly good swimmer, but she had never been in a lake before. When she opened her eyes under the warm water it looked green, with bars of sunlight slanting through it. Tiny seeds floated in it and darting minnows tickled her body. She remembered a book that had frightened her when she was small: *The Tale of Jeremy Fisher*. She couldn't help imagining a huge fish rising up and pulling her under.

After they had rested at the raft, the teenaged girl who was instructing them told them to jump in again. Patricia's feet became tangled in a mass of weeds and she swam up quickly to escape them.

It was a relief when the lesson was finally over. Patricia shivered in a towel and watched Kelly join the White group, the highest level, for her lesson. Now all the mothers decided to go in as well. But instead of swimming, they treaded water in a circle and continued their conversations.

Trevor and Bruce were throwing sticks for Peggy, and Patricia and Christie had been left in charge of the small children. To avoid talking to her cousins, Patricia paddled at the edge of the water and helped a little boy dig a hole. The lake was sudsy where it lapped the shore, and sand bugs hopped in the brown foam. Patricia flicked a speck of mud off her arm. Then she gasped and ran to Christie.

"Something's—something's stuck to me!" Kelly had just returned from her lesson. She and Christie examined Patricia's arm.

"It's a bloodsucker!" said Kelly with relish.

"It'll suck out all your blood if you don't get it off!" added Christie.

Patricia whimpered and pulled at the black dot. It stretched into a revolting worm-like shape, but it wouldn't let go.

"Pull harder," advised Kelly. "Oooh, look how slimy it is, Potty!"

Then Aunt Ginnie was at her side. "Don't be ridiculous, Kelly," she snapped. "You know pulling's no good. Calm down, Patricia, I'll get it off." She picked up a handful of dry sand and dribbled it on the bloodsucker. It curled into a ball and rolled away.

Patricia couldn't keep back her tears. She sniffed and gulped like a baby. Aunt Ginnie tried to soothe her, and the others turned away in disgust. As if she knew Patricia was an outcast, Peggy came up and shook a cold spray over her.

"Potty's a scaredy-cat," whispered Maggie. "*I'm* not afraid of bloodsuckers."

At last it was time for lunch. Everyone carried something up to the carriage and the long procession back to the cottage began. Patricia held her damp towel around her as if it were her misery. She walked wordlessly, surrounded by the chattering family, and thought of two months of mornings like this ahead.

"I've got a plan," Kelly told Trevor after lunch. "We're going to spy on the Cresswells. Come on, Potty," she added in a low voice. "I guess you'll have to come with us."

"Would you like me to help you with Rosemary this afternoon?" Patricia asked her aunt desperately.

"No thank you, dear. She's going down for a nap and I think I'll have one, too."

"I could make dinner if you like," Patricia tried next.

Aunt Ginnie laughed. "You're not here to work, Patricia! You run along and have fun with the others."

Maggie had managed to be included by speeding ahead to Uncle Rod's and meeting them there. Then the six cousins tramped along in the direction of the Main Beach again.

No one spoke to Patricia. By now they must totally despise her, she had proved herself to be such a coward. She wished she could slip away, but where could she go? Her foot caught on a root and she tripped painfully. She didn't dare complain. None of her cousins wore shoes, and this morning Kelly had boasted about how hard the soles of her feet were getting. Even through the thick rubber of her new thongs, Patricia could feel every stone.

She wondered where they were headed. Maybe she could ask Bruce. He was the cousin she was the least afraid of; he was almost as quiet as she was.

"Who are the Cresswells?" Patricia whispered to him.

Kelly heard her. "You'd better learn about them, since you're related to us. Otherwise you'll go leaking information or something. The Cresswells are Other Enders.

That's what we call the kids who live at the other end of the beach—them and the Thorpes and the Vaughns. They're stuck-up and soft and sit around with Walkmans over their ears. They never go fishing or build forts or make fires like we do. Their cottages look like city houses and they have TVs and even VCRs. Except for sailing, they don't know what the lake is *for*."

"Dad says you're a snob when you talk like that," Trevor told his sister. "I wish *we* had TV at the lake."

"You're too dumb to know what you want," Kelly informed him. Trevor shrugged, unconcerned. Every so often he questioned Kelly's bossiness as if it were a matter of principle to do so, but he always gave in without a fight.

"*Our* cottage was one of the first ones on the lake," Kelly continued proudly. "When Mum was little they didn't even have electricity and plumbing. All the cottages at our end are the proper ones."

"Ours is old, too," put in Christie.

"Yes, but not as old as ours … and it's the one where our parents stayed when they were children."

Patricia envied the passion in her cousin's voice when she talked about her family. "My mother went there too," she reminded her timidly.

"I know *that*," Kelly shot back. "There were four children. Uncle Gordon's the oldest—he lives in Victoria now. Then Uncle Rod, your mother and Mum. They sold their share of the cottage to us because your mother and Uncle Gordon didn't live around here anymore, and

Uncle Rod wanted a bigger one. That's why it's all ours," she added with satisfaction.

They had finally reached the other end and, just as Kelly said, the cottages were bigger and more modern, some with painted tubs of flowers in front of them.

"Now here's the plan," said Kelly. "I want to inspect their Laser. We'll sneak along the beach and you can keep watch by the boathouse while I look at it."

At this end, the beach was level with the path. They crept past a red boathouse and huddled in some bushes, while Kelly strolled over to the Cresswells' pier and studied the sailboat lovingly.

"What insect goes skin diving?" Trevor asked after a few minutes.

"A mosquito!" answered Maggie. "I know that one. Why is Kelly taking so long? I don't like sitting in here."

"It's boring," agreed Bruce. "Do you want to go fishing, Trev?"

Christie shifted uncomfortably after the boys had left. "I'm getting cramped. I know, Maggie—let's raid the Vaughns' garden. There may be some carrots. Potty you keep watch until we come back." She and Maggie crawled out and then ran up the beach.

Kelly was inside the sailboat now. She hadn't noticed anyone leave. Patricia was bored, but she was afraid to desert her post. She scratched one of the mosquito bites that dotted her legs. It was chilly in the bushes. She edged farther in to a bare spot and sat down again in the sun-warmed dirt. Bees droned in the still air and a blue dragonfly floated past.

All at once Patricia wondered what her parents were doing. She had been trying her best not to think of them, but sometimes she couldn't help it. They were probably having reasonable discussions about things like how often Patricia would visit her father. When she returned he would be living with Johanna permanently.

Johanna was the woman he had fallen in love with. Patricia had met her only once, at a lunch arranged for this purpose. She was very different from Patricia's mother. Plain, with a gentle face—and quiet, like her father and herself. They had been three shy, silent people, sitting in the Courtyard Café and trying to overcome their embarrassment about the awkward situation they were caught in.

Patricia liked Johanna. She didn't blame her father for wanting to leave them and marry her. She sometimes even envied him for escaping from her mother.

"There's no reason we can't all be sensible about this," her mother kept saying. "Obviously your father"—she no longer referred to him as Harris—"and I can't be together anymore. But you and I will be fine on our own." She said it sternly, as if it were an order.

Patricia could remember when her mother had not been as brittle as she was these days. She had always been domineering, but she used to laugh a lot, as the three of them stripped wallpaper in their old house or went exploring on their bicycles. The more successful her mother became, the more Patricia was awed by her; but it was only this last year, when everything went wrong, that she had begun to feel afraid of her as well.

Now her mother rarely laughed, but she always smiled—a grim, determined, barricading smile.

Patricia's daydreaming was interrupted by a shrill cry: "Hey! What are you doing in our boat?"

Two boys rushed onto the beach. Patricia jumped up and tore out of the bushes in the opposite direction. She caught a glimpse of Kelly running like the wind. She sped ahead and Patricia panted behind her.

"In here!" Kelly hissed. She grabbed Patricia's hand and yanked her so hard her arm felt as if it had been jerked out of its socket. They collapsed in the shrubs by the side of the path. Then Kelly stuck her head out.

"They aren't following us. Probably checking their precious boat to make sure I didn't hurt it." She brushed a few twigs off her pants. "What happened? Where's everyone else? And why didn't you warn me?"

Patricia couldn't look into her cousin's angry face. "They all went away. Trevor and Bruce went fishing, and Christie and Maggie went to pick carrots or something. They left me on guard."

"So why didn't you watch?"

"I … I guess for a minute I wasn't paying attention. I'm sorry."

Kelly clenched her fist. "You are the end, Potty, you really are! You've ruined everything. You have since you got here, and I wish you'd never come!" She pushed through the bushes and disappeared.

Patricia stayed there for a long time, wondering what to do. She couldn't go back to the cottage—Aunt Ginnie would wonder why she was alone. She trudged back to the Grants' beach and sheltered behind the canoe. It felt like her only friend; even though it had dumped her, being in it was the only thing she had enjoyed at the lake so far.

"Loon," she whispered, tracing her fingers over its faded name.

When she thought it was dinnertime, Patricia crept into the cottage and found her cousins playing Monopoly on the verandah. Kelly reddened and turned away. Patricia thought for a second that her cousin looked ashamed, but Kelly had been so angry it was difficult to believe she felt sorry.

After dinner it began to rain. When the baby was asleep Aunt Ginnie read them a chapter from *The Dog Who Wouldn't Be*. Sitting and listening without having to participate felt so safe that Patricia wished her aunt would never stop.

The rain blew in gusts against the windows and the fire crackled and steamed. It was cosy, but Patricia felt so removed from the contented family around her that she almost pinched herself to make sure she was really there.

"Look, Patricia." Aunt Ginnie put the book aside and took down a framed photograph from the mantel. "Here's a picture of your mother at the lake."

The picture was of a strange family group who seemed to be in costume. "We were all dressed in each other's clothes for a party," Aunt Ginnie explained. "I can just remember it. I was Gordon and his pants legs kept coming unrolled and tripping me. The men looked so funny, dressed as Mama and Ruth and me." She was pointing out the faces as she talked. "There's your grand-mother. You'll see her when she comes to stay next week."

"Look how fat you were, Mummy!" crowed Maggie, leaning over Patricia's shoulder.

"You mean you don't think I still am?" teased her mother. "I must have been four then … and Ruth was twelve. Your age, Patricia."

Patricia couldn't stop staring at the photograph. The firelight flickered on its glass, making the faces seem alive. Most of the members of the long-ago family laughed in their silly costumes. All except one, a young girl who glowered between her brothers.

Her mother. Patricia recognized the same fiery eyes, her mother's expression when she was upset about some-thing going wrong with her careful plans. She was dressed in her brother's too-big clothes and looked resentful—as out of place in this cheerful family as Patricia had felt in the photograph in *Toronto Life*.

"We had such happy times," sighed Aunt Ginnie. "That summer the boys were crazy about badminton. They had just finished the court at the back of the cottage, the one that's all overgrown now. Sometimes they tried to teach me to play."

"Were you spoiled, Mummy?" asked Maggie.

"I guess I was a little, Magpie—just like you! It's way past your bedtime."

She and Maggie left the room and Patricia reluctantly replaced the photograph on the mantel. She didn't understand why it had such a hold over her.

"Listen, Potty," said Kelly. "We want to tell you something before Mum comes back."

Patricia waited fearfully.

"You're different from us," began Kelly slowly. She wasn't looking at Patricia, but into the spitting fire. "Even though we're related, you're not the same. It seems to me that if you're going to be with us every day, well ... you don't like playing with us, right?"

Patricia wished it wasn't true, but she nodded.

"But Mum says we have to include you—" said Trevor.

"—so we have a solution," continued Kelly. "Every afternoon we'll pretend to go out together. Then we'll separate. You do what you want and so will we. We'll meet back here for dinner and I guess you'll have to stick with us in the evenings because Mum's around more then. But at least we'll all have our afternoons free and no one will get into trouble. Is it a deal?"

She and Trevor looked almost pleadingly at Patricia. There wasn't any choice. It was obvious they didn't want to be with her, and she didn't want to be with them either. But what was she going to do with herself every afternoon?

"All right," she whispered. "It's a deal."

"Great! It's really for the best, Potty," Kelly sounded almost kind.

"What did one tonsil say to the other?" Trevor asked his sister. They hooted with laughter at the answer.

"That's what I like to hear," said Aunt Ginnie as she came back into the living room. "Everybody having a good time together."

5

*T*he next day after lunch, Kelly scraped back her chair and said cheerfully, "Come on, Patricia. Let's meet the others and start on our fort."

Aunt Ginnie smiled approvingly at her daughter. Patricia wondered what she would think if she could see them a few minutes later. The three cousins stopped walking once they reached the Donaldsons' cottage next door.

"All right, Potty," said Kelly, "when Mum rings the cowbell meet us here."

Patricia glanced at her watch. "What time?"

"*I* don't know," said Kelly scornfully. "I never wear a watch in the summer."

Patricia covered hers up protectively. Her father had given it to her three years ago and it always kept perfect time. She couldn't imagine going through a day without it.

"Just come when you hear the cowbell," Kelly repeated impatiently. She and Trevor ran away and Patricia's first solitary afternoon began.

She spent it sitting by the canoe. At this end of the beach there were more pebbles than sand. Patricia piled them into hills, then listlessly knocked them down again. Late in the afternoon she heard the others swimming from Uncle Rod's raft. She longed to cool off in the lake herself, but she was too frightened of bloodsuckers to go in alone.

The second afternoon it was too hot to stay on the beach. Instead, Patricia explored behind the cottage. Nestled in the woods halfway down the driveway was a tiny guest cabin that the family called La Petite. She opened its door and peeked in.

There was just enough room in the cabin for two narrow beds, a dresser, a rickety chair and a small stove. In one corner lay a pile of old magazines. Patricia kicked off her thongs, curled up on one of the beds and began to leaf through them.

The air in the room was dank, and instead of being too hot Patricia now felt chilled. She dropped the boring magazine on the floor and wrapped the worn chenille bedspread around her.

There was nothing to do in here, but she couldn't think of anywhere else to go. At least it was a safe retreat, even if it was damp and cold. She spotted a few paperbacks beside the other bed and got up to take a look.

"Ouch!" Her own voice startled her; she had stubbed her toe. Squatting to examine it, she noticed a loose board in the uncovered floor. She remembered Uncle Doug mentioning he would be bringing new tiles on the weekend to replace the ones he'd removed last August. The bare floor was grey with age and had a sharp, mouldy smell. Patricia wriggled the loose board, and almost fell backwards as it came up easily.

Underneath was a narrow space. She explored it idly with her fingers. Then she felt a twinge of excitement as she encountered something soft.

Reaching farther into the cavity, she grasped a handful of yellowed cotton cloth. It was rotten, and some pieces fell from it as she lifted it out. Something hard was in the middle. She dug into the bundle and pulled out a round metal object attached to a chain.

It was a thick gold disk with a ring on the top—a pocket watch. Patricia took it back to the bed and examined it. Set in its scratched surface was a glass circle with Roman numerals painted around it. She pressed the knob under the ring, and the top popped open silently, revealing a shiny white face with more numerals and long, delicate, blue-black hands.

She gently snapped the top shut again and turned the watch over. The back had a slightly protruding lip. Sticking her nail under it, she pulled, and another gold surface was exposed, shinier than the outside. Fine writing was inscribed on it; Patricia squinted as she tried to make it out. Then she almost dropped the watch.

"For my dear Patricia, with fondest love from Wilfred."

She pressed the back closed and leaned against the wall, her heart thumping. What was her name doing on a watch? Then she opened it again and relaxed. There was a date underneath the inscription: "August 1929." Of course—Patricia was her grandmother's name, although she'd always been called Pat.

Once Patricia had asked her mother why she had been named after the grandmother she had hardly even seen. "She insisted," her mother had said crisply. "You were the first granddaughter and she wanted the name carried on. And after all, it's my middle name as well as her first one, so it seemed the natural thing to do."

Patricia had always known that her mother and her grandmother didn't get along. Now she wondered what her grandmother was like. This was her watch. "Wilfred" must be the name of her grandfather, who had died long before Patricia could remember.

Surely her grandmother didn't know the watch was here. It looked old and valuable. How had it ended up under the floor? Probably she should show it to Aunt Ginnie. But then she'd have to answer awkward questions about why she wasn't with the others.

The watch cheered her. It fit perfectly into her hand; it had a satisfying weight. For a few seconds she cupped it in her palm, warming the cold metal and running the chain through her fingers.

Its hands pointed to almost two o'clock. That was the same time as on her own watch, so at first she thought it must be working. She held it to her ear to check, but it was silent. Giving the knob three careful turns, she held it up again.

The watch had come to life. Its clear, metallic tick filled the quiet room. Patricia popped open the case again and the ticking became quieter, a tiny even beat. It pleased her enormously.

Then, as abruptly as she had felt a thrill of delight, she felt bleak again. What was she doing huddled inside a cold, dim cabin holding an old watch? "My dear Patricia …" but it wasn't her.

Tears began to well up in her eyes, but she shook her head to stop them. She was tired of feeling so sorry for herself. Aunt Ginnie was right; she had to find something else to think about.

She jumped up, hung the watch around her neck and tucked it under her T-shirt. Warmed by her hands, it was a secret, reassuring weight. Then she burst out of the cabin into the sunlight.

Standing outside the door, she blinked with bewilderment, as if she had been asleep. She had to *do* something. Maybe she could look for the old badminton court Aunt Ginnie had talked about.

Patricia pushed through scratchy bushes and shuffled through mounds of dead leaves. She became hot and dusty but felt slightly better for her exertions. Farther and farther she scrambled into the woods behind the cottage. Then she reached a clearing.

This must be the badminton court, but it wasn't overgrown at all. The grass was clipped smooth and a stiff net stretched over it. Patricia stared at it with surprise.

Her cousins must have done this. They must have been fixing it up secretly when they said they were building a fort. She looked around warily in case they were near.

Loud, ringing voices approached the clearing. Patricia crouched behind some bushes and waited. She would spy on them the way they'd spied on the Cresswells' boat. It was a relief to finally have something to do.

But it wasn't her cousins who stepped onto the grass. What she saw were three strangers—two fair teenaged boys and a young, tall, dark-haired girl.

Patricia recognized them instantly. She had seen those three faces only the night before. I must be asleep, she thought, dizzy with shock. I must be dreaming.

The faces were the ones in the old photograph. Uncle Gordon and Uncle Rod. And Patricia's mother, Ruth.

6

*T*hey were arguing noisily. Patricia watched and listened in a stunned daze.

"You promised I could play too!" shouted Ruth. "It's not fair! I don't want to just keep score."

"Silence, infant," said Gordon, the taller of the two boys. He peeled off a white sweater and unscrewed a press from his badminton racquet. "*After* you keep score, then maybe Rodney and I will let you play."

His sister plopped down by the side of the court, scowling. "Two-love," she muttered, as Rodney missed his brother's serve for the second time.

Patricia couldn't take her eyes away from Ruth. She looked a bit like Kelly, but she was much more striking. Heavy black lashes outlined her large eyes. Her silky hair was held away from her face with a white band. She was dressed in rolled up, baggy jeans and a loose red shirt that emphasized the angry colour in her cheeks.

After Rodney lost the first match, Ruth was allowed to replace him. She whacked the bird across the net and returned Gordon's shots deftly.

"You see?" she puffed when she'd won the first game. "I'm just as good as you two."

"Beginner's luck," said Gordon calmly.

Ping ... ping sang the badminton bird as it whizzed back and forth. Its steady rhythm made Patricia drowse in her hiding place. Dreams were often like this, filled with boring repetition. The scores that Rodney called out were close, but at last Ruth won the match. Then the three of them sprawled on the grass and shared a thermos of something that looked like lemonade.

Patricia wiped the perspiration off her forehead and gazed at the drink longingly. She didn't usually feel so thirsty in dreams, nor so physically present. This wasn't like a dream, and yet it must be—how else could she suddenly be thrust into her mother's past? She felt real enough, however, to want to stay concealed in the bushes.

Ruth and Rodney began another match. She beat him as well, and Patricia cheered silently. Ruth was right: she was just as good as her brothers.

Gordon stood and gazed down at her coolly. "All right, Ruth, you've had a turn with each of us now. Run along so Rodney and I can play seriously."

"We let you beat us, so you should be satisfied," added Rodney.

"Why you—" Ruth sputtered with fury and lifted her racquet as if she wanted to hit the boys with it.

Gordon turned her around by the shoulders and gave her a push. "Don't bother with a tantrum, infant, just leave. After all, Rodney and I made the court."

Ruth opened her mouth, then seemed to decide to be dignified. She marched away but called back, "Father said it was for the whole family. I'll tell on you." Her graceful figure disappeared into the woods.

Patricia decided to follow her. Ruth was much more interesting than the boys. Maybe no one would notice if Patricia stood up, but she didn't want to risk disrupting the dream. Then it might end in the middle, the way dreams so often do. She waited a few minutes, inched backwards cautiously then pushed through the trees until she reached La Petite again.

As she came around the corner of the cabin she brushed herself off, marvelling again that her hot, grimy body felt so real. Then she halted in shock.

A huge car stood in the driveway: a grey bubble shape with enormous fenders and oval windows. The Alberta licence plates were dated thirty-five years earlier—exactly the year that her mother would have been twelve.

Surely people dreamed about what they knew. Patricia didn't know what cars looked like thirty-five years ago. Everything was becoming too detailed, too logical for a dream. But she pushed the uncomfortable thought away. It made her head ache to try to figure it out. She didn't want it to end, dream or not. It was the most interesting thing that had ever happened to her.

She headed on to the front of the cottage, where she heard voices. One was Ruth's. Feeling unusually brave, Patricia took a deep breath and crept around the corner of the verandah. She hid behind the front steps and watched the scene before her with rivetted attention.

"But Mother, it's supposed to be for all of us!" Ruth stood in front of a languid figure stretched out on a chaise lounge on the lawn. The woman's brown hair was puffed around a pinched face. Her eyes were narrow and she had a long, crooked mouth painted very red. Her pink gingham dress was pulled up to let the sun on her legs. She held open a book called *The Whiteoaks of Jalna* and she glanced up reluctantly as if the story was pulling her back down.

This must be my grandmother! Patricia calculated rapidly and remembered the inscription. She clutched the watch as she listened, its steady beat vibrating through the thin material of her T-shirt.

Pat Reid's voice sounded distant. "Ruth, I am so tired of listening to you complain about the badminton court. They let you have a turn, didn't they?"

"Yes, but—"

Ruth's mother interrupted her as she turned back to her book. "That's enough," she murmured without looking up. "Gordon and Rodney don't want their little sister around them *all* the time. It was kind of them to let you play wasn't it?"

"But Father said—"

"Leave me alone, please, Ruth. Your father's visiting next door and Ginnie's asleep. I was hoping for an hour to myself."

"I'll go and tell Father, then, if you won't listen," mumbled Ruth, so softly that only Patricia heard her.

"Maaamaaa … I want to get up!" A child's shrill voice came from the cottage.

Pat Reid sighed and turned over her novel. "There's Ginnie, awake already."

Ruth began to edge away but her mother stopped her. "Wait, Ruth. Since you're so restless you can get Ginnie up and take her to the Main Beach."

"Oh, Mother!" Ruth slapped a bush with her badminton racquet. "It's not fair! I always have to look after her, and Gordon and Rodney never do!"

Patricia was startled when Ruth's mother suddenly lost her lazy manner. Her homely face filled with colour and her eyes darkened as she sat up and directed them upon her daughter. It was as if she had become someone else.

"You listen to me, young lady! I don't know what's got into you this summer. Ever since we arrived you've done nothing but complain. Now, either you fetch Ginnie immediately or you go to your room for the rest of the afternoon."

Ruth's grey eyes flickered with fear at her mother's sharp tone, but they returned her gaze steadily. "I'd much rather go to my room," she answered. Before her mother could answer she flounced into the cottage, slamming the screen door behind her.

A plump, pigtailed child, dressed only in white underpants, pushed through the door and trotted across the grass. "Mama, didn't you hear me? I want to get up now!"

Patricia couldn't help smiling. Aunt Ginnie as a little girl was exactly the same as she was as an adult. The same round face, the same placid movements. She clambered onto her mother with difficulty.

"Why is Ruthie mad? She shut her door very hard."

Pat Reid hugged Ginnie. "What a lump you are, sweetheart! Ruth has been a bad girl and she's gone to her room." Her anger had dissolved; the nonchalant woman Patricia had first seen had returned.

"*I'm* not a bad girl." Ginnie started bouncing on her mother's stomach.

"No, you're my little angel, aren't you? But get off Mama, you're too heavy. Look, there's your ball."

Ginnie rolled off but continued to chatter. The indulgent, amused way in which Pat Reid answered her was so different from the chilly tone she had used with Ruth. It puzzled Patricia.

She had been crouching so long that her body was cramped. She sat down and stretched out her legs, leaning against the side of the steps. Then, without warning, a beach ball bounced towards her and stopped in front of her feet. Before she had time to act, Ginnie had run up behind it.

Patricia gasped as the little girl bent to pick up the ball. But Ginnie didn't see her. She looked right at Patricia as if through air, then ran back to the lawn.

The dream was getting better all the time. Now it seemed she was invisible! She stood up and forced her trembling legs over to stand in front of her grandmother. Pat Reid continued to look at Ginnie.

If they couldn't see her, they probably couldn't hear her either. "Hello," said Patricia softly. Then, louder, "Hello! Hello, Aunt Ginnie and my grandmother!"

Ginnie's mother shivered and rubbed her daughter's back. "Are you warm enough, sweetheart?"

Patricia danced the pins and needle out of her legs. They couldn't see or hear her. In everyday life she had often wished she could be invisible. Now she really was.

It was a powerful position. Nobody could bother her. Nobody's attention could be drawn to her awkward presence. She didn't have to be afraid to do anything wrong, she didn't have to think of anything to say. She felt so safe, she hoped she wouldn't wake up for a long time.

For the rest of the afternoon, Patricia explored the inside of the cottage. Ginnie and her mother had gone to the beach, but she preferred to stay near Ruth. It was tempting to open the bedroom door and peek in—she was sure Ruth wouldn't be able to see her either. A door opening on its own might scare her, though.

The cottage looked almost same with its rag rugs and wicker furniture, although the colours were brighter and the paint wasn't peeling. There was no electric stove, refrigerator or bathroom: Patricia wondered what the family did without them.

Gordon and Rodney came back and left again in funny bathing suits that looked like patterned, baggy shorts. Then the whole family came back to the cottage at the same time.

Pat Reid walked briskly across the living room and knocked on Ruth's door. "All right, Ruth, you can come out now." There was no response. Not until Ruth's father appeared did Ruth open the door, slouch behind a card table on the verandah and start to work on a jigsaw puzzle.

It was spooky to see Mr. Reid. In real life he was dead. Patricia recognized his white moustache and hooked nose from the photograph. Everyone deferred to him. Gordon and Rodney called him "sir," and his wife brought him a drink and his pipe once he had established himself in his rocking chair. Only Ginnie seemed to relax in his presence. She curled up on her father's lap while he and his wife sipped their drinks and talked.

Patricia sat on the verandah and watched the boys play chess. She couldn't resist moving one of Rodney's pieces when he wasn't looking and chuckled at the argument that followed. She was tempted to help Ruth with her puzzle, but she didn't want to tease her the way she had teased Rodney.

When it was time for dinner, the children waited quietly while their father carved a large roast. Nobody reached or giggled, as Kelly, Trevor and Maggie did at this same table. Patricia perched on the windowsill, getting very hungry at the sight of the succulent beef. Aunt Ginnie had just said this morning that she wished they could afford a roast more often.

Ruth kept glancing at her father as if bursting to bring up the subject of badminton. He finally mentioned it himself. "How's the new court working out?" he asked, after he had told them they could begin.

Gordon swallowed before he replied. "It's fine, sir. Almost as good as at the club in town, although the wind might be a challenge. Would you like to play tomorrow?"

"Oh, I think my badminton days are over." For the first time, Patricia noticed how much older he was than his wife.

"Father," said Ruth, laying down her knife and fork, "didn't you say the badminton court was for all of us?"

"Now, Ruth," warned her mother, but Ruth ignored her and continued.

"Gordon and Rodney only let me play twice, and then they made me leave. And I'm just as good as they are, too."

Rodney glared at her, then appealed to his father. "But *we* cleared the bushes last August and mowed the grass yesterday. It's really ours. She can play once in a while, but we won't get enough practice if we always have to go easy for her. I'd like to get on the club team in the fall." Gordon nodded in agreement.

Their father wiped his moustache carefully "I'm afraid the boys have a point, Ruth. They did do all the work—"

"—because they wouldn't let me help!"

"Don't interrupt, young lady. Gordon and Rodney can play one match with you a day. The rest of the time it's theirs. They're growing boys and they need the exercise. *You* need to spend more time helping your mother. I hear you refused to look after your little sister today. I don't want to hear any more reports like that, do you understand?"

"Yes, Father," said Ruth stiffly. She looked as if she wanted to say more but didn't dare.

"*I* want to play ba'minton," piped up Ginnie. "Can I?"

Everyone except Ruth laughed. "Sure you can, baby," said Gordon. "I'll teach you tomorrow."

After dinner Rodney and Gordon were sent outside to chop kindling. Ruth had to help her mother heat water on the wood stove and wash the dishes. The atmosphere between the two of them was so tense that Patricia was relieved when Pat Reid sent Ruth and Rodney to the store.

"I can go alone," Ruth said.

"You can't fill all the water bottles by yourself. Don't be so stubborn. And don't hang around, either. Your father wants his paper."

A few minutes later, Patricia followed Ruth and her brother as they pulled a wagon containing large brown bottles along the road behind the cottage. It wasn't tarred the way it was in real life. Now it was just loose, dry dirt.

The bottles rattled against each other and the wagon wheels creaked and churned up dust. Then Ruth spoke. "I've decided I'm not going to play badminton at all this summer. It would just get boring, winning all the time."

Good for her, thought Patricia.

Rodney shrugged. "Suits me. You're just being a poor sport, though."

Patricia hadn't been paying much attention to Rodney in this dream. Now she examined him more closely. He and Gordon looked and acted a lot alike; they were both blond and arrogant. But where Gordon was sure of himself, Rodney was defensive, as if he were not quite sure of his superiority and had to prove it all the time.

When they reached the store they stopped at a green metal pump. Ruth stood one of the wide-mouthed bottles under its spout as Rodney worked the handle. The iron parts screeched and rattled, but at first no water came out. Then it gushed forth.

"Let me do it," insisted Ruth.

"You're not strong enough."

"Of course I am!" Ruth pushed her brother aside and grabbed the handle. When the bottle was full, Rodney lifted it back into the wagon and took out another.

After they had filled them all and stopped pumping, the water continued to flow. Ruth and Rodney each stuck their red faces under the spout. Then Patricia, too, thrust her head into the stream and opened her mouth. Icy water ran over her face and hair. It jolted her into an alertness that seemed much too real for a dream. The water was delicious, tinny and sharp. She drank deeply until the gush became a trickle, her feet slipping on the wet wooden platform. Then she ran to catch up with the others.

The store was crowded with children and teenagers. They sat, reading comics and chewing bubble gum, on a bench that edged the windows. Rodney swaggered in front of a group of girls while Ruth bought a paper, bread and milk. Then he sauntered back to her.

"Listen, Ruth. The Thorpes are having a marshmallow roast. Can you manage the wagon alone? You did say you could do it by yourself," he reminded her. "When you get home tell Mother and Father I won't be too late, and ask Gordon to come."

"I don't see why I should," retorted Ruth. She eyed the giggling girls suspiciously. "You're only fifteen, you know. I bet Mother won't like you going to a mixed party."

"It's only a marshmallow roast," said Rodney, flushing. "Just do as I say. Look, I'll give you a quarter if you will."

Ruth pocketed the money. "All right, but don't blame me if you get into trouble."

She had a hard time pulling the heavy wagon back to the cottage. The full bottles jiggled and spilled water on the bumpy road. Patricia tried pushing and grinned at Ruth's surprise when her task became easier.

Gordon helped her carry the water into the kitchen. "Rodney's gone to a marshmallow roast at the Thorpes," Ruth told him.

"The Thorpes?" said Gordon eagerly. Patricia followed him into the living room as he handed his father the newspaper and asked if he could go as well.

"Are their parents going to be there?" said his mother. "I know what these parties turn into at your age. Rodney should have come home and asked."

"Please, Ma," begged Gordon.

Mr. Reid put down his pipe. He smiled under his moustache. "It's those young Thorpe girls, isn't it, Gordon? I saw them today … they're turning into attractive young ladies. All right, son, but be home by eleven."

"Andrew, I still don't think—" his wife protested as Gordon hurried out.

"Now, Pat, they have to grow up sometime."

She sighed, pulled the kerosene lamp closer and picked up a scrapbook she was working on.

Ruth stood in the doorway. "May I take the canoe out?"

Her mother frowned. "At this time of night?"

"It's not dark yet."

"Oh, all right."

"Pull it well up when you come in," added her father. The two of them seemed impatient to settle down to a quiet evening and didn't look up as Ruth, followed by Patricia, left the cottage.

Something nudged Patricia's mind as she followed Ruth down to the beach. Her grandmother had called her husband Andrew. But wasn't his name Wilfred? That was the name on the watch.

This is a *dream*, she reminded herself. It doesn't have to make sense. It occurred to her, however, that in dreams everything made sense. It was in reality that you noticed when something didn't.

Once down at the beach she didn't have time to ponder any more. She had to concentrate on getting into the canoe safely. It was hard to believe it was the same boat she had fallen out of just a few days ago. Its green paint was glossier, but the same crooked letters saying *Loon* were painted on its prow.

As she settled herself on the floor her hand bumped against Ruth's knee. She froze in panic, but Ruth simply scratched her leg as if a fly had landed on it.

Patricia faced Ruth as the tall, dark girl steered the canoe. She was just as good at it as Kelly. Patricia studied her carefully and imitated the movements of her arms.

Ruth's paddle dripped into water turned pink by the setting sun. Then an eerie cry came across the lake. It sounded like a mournful yodel—some kind of bird, Patricia guessed.

Ruth had tears in her eyes. They beaded on her thick lashes and slid down her face. Patricia's own eyes prickled in sympathy. If only this weren't a dream and she weren't invisible, she could talk to this solitary girl. But all she could do was stare at her loneliness.

The bird called again. With a sigh, Ruth wiped the back of her hand across her eyes. "I'll show them," she whispered. "Someday I'll show them all."

She turned the boat towards the shore, but Patricia never got there. One instant she was in the canoe. The next, she was sitting on the bed in La Petite.

7

*P*atricia ran her hands rapidly over the tufted pattern of the chenille bedspread. She couldn't believe that she was back here so suddenly … that the vivid dream was over. She rubbed her forehead, trying to wake up fully.

Her hair was damp.

She pulled her fingers through it and started to tremble. Her hair was damp because an hour ago she had stuck her head under icy water that had seemed surprisingly real.

Had it been real? She had been just as wide awake then as she was now. She had known it all along in some part of her. Pretending it was a dream had cushioned the shock of what had happened—that, somehow, she had been spirited back thirty-five years to her mother's childhood and now, just as mysteriously, had returned to the present.

Think it out, she told herself dizzily. There must be a logical explanation. That was one of her mother's favourite phrases.

How long had she been gone? It had been about two when she had left the cabin. She looked at her wristwatch and shook it. The hands still pointed to two o'clock; the battery must have run down.

Then she took out the other watch, the gold one hidden under her T-shirt. It said nine thirty-five.

The second hand on her own watch was still jerking forward. It hadn't run down after all. But the pocket watch had stopped. She pressed it to her ear, but there was no sound.

Patricia lay down on her back on the bed, her fingers running along the watch's gold chain. She sat up again with excitement as the solution came to her.

It was the watch. She had wound it up and it had taken her back to 1949. It had carried on ticking away the seconds and minutes and hours of the time it had kept when it was last wound. Then it had run down, so the other time had ended and her own time, 1984, had started again where she had left it—at two o'clock.

It *was* a logical explanation; all except for the reason it had happened. But Patricia was too exhilarated to worry about why. She knew it had happened—her wet hair was proof. And it could happen again. She was certain that, if she wanted to go back to Ruth's time, all she had to do was rewind the watch.

She couldn't do it yet, although she knew she would later. Right now she needed some time to recover. At least she had plenty of it. She'd spent about seven hours in the past, but in the present she still had the whole afternoon to lie and think.

She curled up and pondered every detail of the adventure. Her grandparents, Pat and Andrew. (Why not Wilfred?) Her uncles, Gordon and Rodney. Her aunt,

Ginnie. And especially Ruth, her mother. Ruth's anger and isolation and unhappiness. And old cars and wood stoves and pumps and the canoe and the strange call of a bird ... Patricia closed her eyes.

Ding! Ding! Ding! The clear peal of a cowbell startled her awake. Feeling very tired and confused, Patricia checked her wristwatch: five o'clock. She was here, in the present, and she had to meet Kelly and Trevor and pretend she'd been with them the whole afternoon.

First she had to hide the pocket watch. She lifted it off her neck and caressed its smooth surface for a second. She didn't want to return it to the cavity beneath the floorboard in case Uncle Doug put down the new tiles. Glancing around the room, she quickly thrust the watch under the mattress of the bed she'd been lying on. She balled up the yellowed cotton and pushed that under the mattress, too. Then she ran out of the cabin.

Patricia yawned all through dinner. "Are you all right?" Aunt Ginnie asked her. "What did you three do this afternoon?"

Her aunt looked surprised and pleased when her niece grinned at her. It was impossible to believe Aunt Ginnie was grown up, she still looked so much like her four-year-old self. "We ... ummm ... built a fort," Patricia answered, noting Kelly's relieved expression.

Aunt Ginnie sent her to bed early. She stretched, luxuriously alone, in the cosy sheets. This had been Ruth's room, too; maybe even her bed. It was a comforting thought.

THE NEXT MORNING Patricia again contrived to go to the Main Beach with Aunt Ginnie. As they waited for the others to join them, she cleared her throat and asked a tentative question.

"Aunt Ginnie … about my grandmother's husband …"

"Call her Nan, Patricia!" laughed her aunt. "I know you haven't seen her for years, but she'd want you to call her what the others do."

"Yes, well … Nan's husband. What was his name?"

"Andrew."

"What was his middle name?" Surely it was Wilfred.

"He had two: Thomas and Hughes. Andrew Thomas Hughes Reid. Father was quite pompous. Having three names suited him. But why do you want to know?"

Patricia babbled an answer. "I just wondered. He died before I was born, didn't he? What was he like?"

She barely listened to Aunt Ginnie's reply because she already knew what he was like. But she still didn't know who Wilfred was.

"Father could be terrifying. He made a pet of me when I was little, but later on I was frightened of him. He was one of those people who grow more rigid with age. And he was quite a bit older than Mama, you know. I sometimes wonder if she only married him because …"

"Because why?" prompted Patricia, now interested again. It was so convenient, the way Aunt Ginnie was willing to gossip about the Reids. She could learn a lot.

"Because she was trying to recover from losing her first fiancé. Mama was engaged to Father's younger brother, but he died of polio, which was a common disease in those days. She loved him very much—she's talked about him to me. She still does, sometimes. I think she never got over him."

"What was—what was his name?" asked Patricia, guessing the answer.

"Wilfred. Now, that's a name you never hear anymore. Maggie, no! You're too far out!" Aunt Ginnie jumped up and ran down to the water.

Patricia sat dreamily on her towel. That explained why the watch was inscribed with the name Wilfred. But how did it come to be hidden under the floor? If she kept visiting the past, maybe she would find out. It was like reading an incredibly absorbing book; she wanted to discover all she could about the Reids.

Rosemary cooed beside her and Patricia picked her up, holding her hand behind the baby's neck the way Aunt Ginnie had shown her. Rosemary was a silky warm lump. Her hair smelled like vanilla. She blew a raspberry at Patricia—her latest trick—and Patricia blew one back. She hoisted the fat baby over her shoulder and held her close, as if she were guarding her secret. This afternoon she would wind the watch and go back again.

BUT AFTER LUNCH Aunt Ginnie had other plans. "Patricia, dear, do you feel ready to learn how to paddle the canoe? The lake's so calm today it would be a good time for Kelly to give you a lesson."

Both Patricia and Kelly looked crestfallen, but Aunt Ginnie stilled their objections. "It's something you should know, Patricia. Don't you want to learn?"

She did—though not this afternoon. But there was nothing she could do about it. They had to gather up paddles and life jackets and carry them down to the beach.

"Don't you dare work on the fort without me!" Kelly shouted after Trevor, who pushed past them on the path.

"We can if we want to!" he yelled back.

"I hope you're a fast learner," Kelly muttered as she tugged the canoe across the pebbles. "Then we can waste just one afternoon on this. They'll ruin that fort without me."

Once Patricia had resigned herself to having a canoe lesson, she began to enjoy it. Kelly didn't know she had been observing someone paddle only yesterday.

"Don't sit—kneel with your legs apart and lean against the thwart," commanded Kelly. "That's right." She looked surprised when her cousin immediately took the correct position in the bow Patricia picked up her paddle and put her right hand over the top and her left one around the middle. When Kelly pushed off, she slipped the paddle in the water and lifted it out. The canoe moved forward.

"Hey! I thought you didn't know how to do this! You sure couldn't when you dumped it. Has someone else been teaching you?" Kelly looked suspicious.

Patricia flushed. "I've been watching you from the shore." Again she dipped in her paddle the way she'd copied Ruth. It made only a slight splash.

"That's pretty good," said Kelly grudgingly. "You catch on fast. Don't put it in so deep and try to get a rhythm. *One* two, *one* two …"

With both of them paddling, the canoe glided so swiftly that it left a gurgling wake behind. Then Kelly showed Patricia how to turn her paddle for the "J" stroke. "That's how I steer. Then it doesn't matter which side you paddle on. Here, I'll stop and we'll switch positions. You steer now."

Carefully they turned in their places so that Patricia was now facing Kelly's back. It was difficult to stop the boat from going in a circle, but eventually she was able to keep it on a fairly straight course.

"You're really doing well!" Kelly's expression was one of undisguised admiration. Then she looked embarrassed, as if she hadn't meant to sound so friendly. "Next time, Potty, I'll let you try taking it out alone. Let's switch again. I'll take us to the Main Beach and back."

All the way there Patricia matched her strokes to her cousin's. Every time she lifted up her paddle it left spinning whorls in the water. Her arm was getting sore, but she kept going. I can paddle a canoe! she thought. Like Kelly … like Ruth.

"Why is this canoe called the *Loon*?" she asked.

"Because loons come here. Our grandparents must have named it—it's a really old canoe. Christie and Bruce's is lighter, but this one's steadier."

"What do loons look like?"

"Don't you know?" A trace of familiar scorn came back into Kelly's voice. "Loons are wonderful—big birds with black heads and speckled bands around their necks. They used to nest on this lake but now it's too noisy, so they just come here to feed. You hear them mostly at night. They sound like they're laughing. That's why people say someone's loony. It's a weird, laughing sound."

But beautiful, too, Patricia remembered. She wished she were in the canoe with Ruth again. She wondered what Ruth was doing. Being in the *Loon* with Kelly, who looked like Ruth but wasn't, made her long for the other girl.

THAT EVENING Aunt Ginnie sent them to the store as usual to get the paper. On the way they called on Christie and Bruce. Patricia cringed when Uncle Rod came into the backyard and boomed a greeting.

"Well, here's our little Easterner! Why are you still so white, when the others are as brown as berries?"

"I don't know," whispered Patricia. She examined him fearfully. All that was left of his boyhood hair was a grey fringe above his ears. His expression was still patronizing; he looked at her in the present the way he did at Ruth in the past.

"Ready to show me your teeth, now?" Uncle Rod loomed over her.

"Daddy, we have to go!" said Christie impatiently. Patricia scuttered down the driveway after her cousins.

When they neared the store she looked around eagerly for the pump. It was still there, but it was rusty and half-buried in weeds.

"Does that old pump still work?" she asked Bruce.

"No," Kelly answered for him. "They boarded up the well years ago because the water was contaminated."

Patricia walked on sadly, her mouth recalling the water's tang. Then she brightened, remembering that she could go back and taste it again.

The Other Enders were sitting around the store. They read comics and chewed gum just as they had thirty-five years ago. Two of them even resembled the Thorpe girls from the past. For an instant Patricia forgot what time she was in.

Kelly walked by the group without a word.

"Hey, Kelly!" called one of the Cresswell boys, putting down his comic. His sister stared haughtily at them.

"What you want?" Kelly said coolly.

"Just to remind you to leave our boat alone or I'll tell my parents."

"Don't worry," retorted Kelly. "I wouldn't touch your stupid boat. I just wanted to see how flimsy it was and I was right."

Her words sounded lame. The row of eyes observed her with pity, then dropped to their reading.

"Somehow we've got to get them!" said Kelly on the way home. "They're one up on us now."

Patricia sighed guiltily; Kelly was probably remembering how she had let her down at the Cresswells.

Maggie ran to catch up with them. "Look what I found!" Around her neck curled a striped snake. Its tongue darted in and out rapidly as Trevor held it up.

"Look, Potty!" He waved it in her face. "Do you like garter snakes?"

"P-please don't!" gasped Patricia. She slowed her steps and let her cousins walk ahead. Their laughter floated back and the familiar feeling of isolation filled here again.

Then she remembered her secret. Tomorrow, she thought. Tomorrow I'll go back again.

8

*I*f she was right about the watch keeping its own time, it should take her back to exactly the same minute she had left: nine thirty-five in the evening. Patricia's fingers trembled as she sat on the bed in La Petite and twisted the gold knob. She decided to wind it more tightly so she could stay in the past longer.

She closed her eyes, expecting to be transported to the canoe. But she opened them on the same setting. The watch had resumed its brisk ticking, but she was still in the cabin, not out on the lake with Ruth.

It hadn't worked. Almost in tears, Patricia jumped up and paced the floor frantically. The space was too small to contain her frustration; she pushed open the door of the cabin and stumbled out.

Dusk greeted her: a hushed evening with a few stars dotting the sky. The old-fashioned car in the driveway loomed mysteriously in the dim light.

It *had* worked. Patricia tucked the watch inside her shirt, shivering with relief and excitement. She had come back, and she could stay here until the watch ran down again. She hurried to the front of the cottage to look for Ruth.

The *Loon* was gliding to shore. With a slight crunch it reached the beach, just as Pat Reid opened the door of the cottage.

"Ruth! Come in at once!"

"Coming," answered a sullen voice below.

When Ruth appeared, her eyes were still glistening with tears. Patricia felt as if she had stopped a movie, then started it again two days later.

They went inside the cottage and Ruth was sent to bed. With dismay, Patricia realized that now she had the whole night to get through. She couldn't make the watch skip time. It ticked out every long minute and she would have to endure each one until morning.

For a while she was occupied with watching Ruth's parents. Peering over Pat Reid's shoulder, she saw that the scrapbook she was working on was about the Royal Family. "HRH Princess Elizabeth plays with HRH Prince Charles," read the caption under a photograph she snipped out of the newspaper. In it, a pretty young woman held up a solemn-looking baby with large ears.

Shortly after the grown-ups went to bed, Gordon and Rodney arrived home. Gordon was laughing, but Rodney sulked and seemed resentful of his brother's good mood.

"Go to bed, you two," called their father. They tramped up the kitchen stairs to the attic.

Patricia continued to look for ways to pass the time. First she crept around the cottage, peeking in at Ginnie, clutching a doll, and Ruth, twisted awkwardly in her sheets. Then she fitted together a few pieces in Ruth's jigsaw puzzle. She sat on the verandah and stared at the moon's path on the lake, while the cottage full of sleeping Reids breathed peacefully. If only she could shout and wake them all up.

Finally Patricia decided to try to sleep herself. She wasn't at all tired, but she would be later, especially when she got back to the present. Stretching out on a cot on the verandah, she tried counting sheep.

She tossed for hours. Her mind kept reviewing all the things that had happened during this strange summer. For the first time in days, she remembered her parents' separation. Why couldn't morning come so she wouldn't have to think? This night was so boring, she almost wished she were back in the present, but the watch ticked out its own time relentlessly. Patricia felt trapped, knowing she couldn't return until it stopped. The watch pulsed on her chest chest like a second heart drowning out her own.

A LONG TIME LATER she sat up abruptly, shaking off a dream about her parents. What was she doing on the verandah? For a few seconds she forgot she was still in the past. Then she heard again the whisper that had awakened her.

"Hurry up, Ruth!" Rodney was in the living room. As Patricia stood up sleepily Ruth tiptoed out of her room, pulling on a sweater. They brushed past her—Patricia shuddered because she didn't feel anything—and collected fishing equipment and oars from the verandah.

It was surprising to see the two of them going somewhere together after their arguing yesterday.

The sun was barely up. Patricia checked the watch: five o'clock. She couldn't remember ever being out this early in the morning. The air had a bite to it and the sun glinted off the poplar leaves. Birds competed in a deafening, joyful chorus. Patricia breathed in the crisp air thirstily and swung her arms to warm up, flicking aside the spider webs that stretched across the path. Everything was new; best of all was this new day with the family she was becoming so attached to.

Down at the beach, Rodney overturned a small grey rowboat shaped like a nutshell. Patricia got into it gingerly and scrambled up to the bow. The rowboat felt much more stable than the canoe, but it didn't come alive in the water in the same way; and it didn't have a name.

Ruth rowed energetically while Rodney fixed lures onto the fishing lines. Then they dropped the oars and began to cast.

The sun was getting warmer. Patricia stopped shivering and stretched out her bare legs. For the first time, she noticed there was no power plant spoiling the horizon.

"Thanks for coming out," Rodney told his sister gruffly. "We can catch more with two of us."

Ruth didn't seem surprised, as Patricia was, at his friendly tone. So they weren't always enemies. Patricia didn't want to revise her opinion of Rodney, but he was different this morning. His face looked younger as he flung out his line again and again.

"Got one!" he said eagerly. He reeled in quickly as Ruth held out a net. She scooped up a wriggling striped fish about six inches long.

It was a perch. Patricia knew that, because Trevor had brought one in yesterday. He had insisted on Aunt Ginnie cooking it for breakfast, even though it made barely a mouthful. It had been his first fish of the summer.

But now Ruth got a strike, then another, then Rodney caught three in a row. Soon the bucket at the bottom of the boat was half full of flopping silver shapes. Patricia watched the fish with interest and reached out to touch one. It felt cold and slimy but not nearly as horrible as she had expected.

"How was the marshmallow roast?" Ruth asked her brother.

Rodney flushed as red as he had at the store. "It was boring. Those girls are stupid."

"Did Gordon like it?"

"Oh, him … they all think he's so wonderful, just because he's old enough to drive."

Patricia guessed what she knew Ruth was thinking— that Rodney had only been asked to the roast so that Gordon would come.

"Never mind," said Ruth. "They *are* dumb."

"I'll play you a game of badminton after breakfast," her brother offered.

Ruth's face closed. "No thanks—I told you I wasn't playing anymore and I'm not."

She changed the subject as she pointed to shore. "Look! Indians on horses!" The three of them watched some distant figures gallop around the point and disappear.

Ruth sighed. "I *wish* Mother would let me rent a horse from them."

"You know you shouldn't associate with the Indians. They're lazy and dirty."

"They're not!" said Ruth indignantly. "You're just copying what Father says. He's not always right, you know."

Rodney shrugged. "I think we've got enough fish now." Ruth rowed in, but not to the Reids' beach, as Patricia expected. Instead she steered to a wooded area near the point.

"We shouldn't land here," said Rodney uneasily. "It's part of the Reserve."

"I don't think the Indians would mind," said Ruth. "And Mother and Father will never know."

She jumped out and in a few minutes had a small fire started in the sand; soon a dozen perch were sizzling over it. The smell was overwhelmingly tantalizing and Patricia was faced with a dilemma. She had to taste one of those crisp brown morsels, but how? She pictured Ruth and Rodney seeing a fish rise on its own out of the pan.

Then she had an idea. Picking up a rock behind their backs, she threw it into the water. When they turned their heads she snatched up a perch.

"Ouch!" cried Patricia. Her burnt fingers dropped the fish into the sand. She brushed it off and crammed it into her mouth before the others turned around.

"What was that?"

"A fish jumped, I guess," shrugged Rodney.

"No, it was a duck or something. I heard it call, didn't you?"

Rodney shook his head as he divided up the fish. "You ate one!" he accused her.

"No, I didn't!"

"You must have. There's only eleven and we cleaned twelve."

"You probably counted wrong," said Ruth, gobbling up her share of the fish as fast as they cooled.

THEY ARRIVED BACK at the cottage in time for breakfast. "Ruth Reid, just look at you!" scolded her mother.

Ruth's hands and face were smeared with butter and soot; sand, blood and scales caked her clothes. "Rodney looks just as bad," she muttered.

Patricia cringed, expecting the same outburst as yesterday. But today Pat Reid's voice was simply irritated.

"Rodney is a boy. You're a girl—too old to be acting like a hoyden. Now clean up quickly and help me with breakfast."

Patricia had her own breakfast in the kitchen, after she found cookies and fruit in a large pantry—the room that was the bathroom in the present. She had found out what they did without a bathroom when she heard Pat Reid sending Ginnie to the outhouse.

After breakfast Patricia walked to the Main Beach with Ruth and Ginnie. She remembered Aunt Ginnie saying how much Ruth must have resented taking her there every day. Sure enough, a sulky expression was on Ruth's face.

There were no swimming lessons going on, but the raft and pier were the same and the sand was even more crowded with families. The women were dressed in bunchy cotton bathing suits and they all wore caps in the water.

Patricia dozed in the sun and listened to the ring of metal upon metal that came from a group of men throwing horseshoes at a pole. A cairn terrier approached her and sniffed suspiciously. It cocked its head, puzzled that there was no body to match the smell.

Patricia shivered as it ran away. What an odd sensation it was both to be and not to be here. She wondered how much time she had left.

Maybe she didn't have to wait for the watch to run down; maybe she could rewind it now and stay longer. Her fingers twisted the knob, but it wouldn't budge. Alarmed that she'd broken it, Patricia held the gold disk to her ear, but it ticked on reassuringly. The knob must be stuck, or maybe it only moved after the ticking stopped. She would have to wait until then and try again.

Now she began to dread the shock of being whisked back. Then a boy who was talking to Ruth distracted her.

"Where are your brothers?" he asked. He looked about Rodney's age.

"Playing badminton," said Ruth. "They're *always* playing badminton. If you want a game, Tom, they'll be on the court until lunch."

"That's okay—I'd rather talk to you." He sat down beside her and began boasting about his father's motorboat. He had curly black hair and a wide grin and he was showing off.

Showing off to get Ruth's attention; flirting with her. Ruth looked older than her age and she was easily the prettiest girl on the beach. Patricia watched, fascinated.

Ruth seemed surprised and bewildered at Tom's attention; then she put on the aloof expression she used with her brothers.

"Have you heard about the costume party there's going to be at the rec hall?" Tom asked her. "The second-last Saturday in July. Do you think you'll be going?"

Ruth shrugged.

"Everyone will be there," Tom continued. "Would you like to go with me?"

"I don't go out on dates. Come on, Ginnie, it's time for lunch."

"Well, let me know if you change your mind. See you." The boy whistled as he walked away.

Patricia was impressed. A few of the girls in her class already went out with boys, but nobody had ever asked her. She writhed with shyness at the possibility.

But Ruth was different—she was beautiful. How strange it must be just to be sitting on a towel and have a boy come up and flirt. Strange and uncomfortable; she didn't blame Ruth for refusing his offer. It must feel powerful, though, to have a choice.

"Hurry up, Ginnie!" Ruth sighed as her small sister stopped on the path to examine her foot.

"I stubbed my toe-oe, Ruthie," the child wailed. "You have to carry me …"

The rest of her complaint was cut off as Patricia found herself back in La Petite.

9

*Q*uickly she pulled out the watch. Oh. please don't still be stuck, she prayed. But before her fingers had a chance to try the knob, a voice called outside.

"Pawwwty …" Patricia just had time to slip the watch under her shirt before her five cousins burst into the cabin.

"Here you are!" Kelly looked at Patricia curiously. "I wondered where you spent your time. Listen, Potty, you have to come with us."

Patricia stared at them blearily. The only place she wanted to go was right back to Ruth; and she didn't even know if the watch was broken.

"We're going on a picnic," Kelly continued. "Mum's packing it now. You have to come or she'll suspect something. Potty, are you listening? Have you been asleep?"

"I'm going, too," said Maggie proudly. "Mum said they had to take me."

"So come *on*," urged Christie. "The food must be ready."

Patricia gathered herself together. "I'll catch up with you in a few minutes," she said slowly. After they had left she hid the watch under the mattress again. It would just have to wait for her until tomorrow; or maybe she could sneak away tonight.

Back at the cottage Aunt Ginnie handed them two bulging knapsacks. "Your sweaters and bathing suits are in one. I put in extras for you and Bruce, Christie. You must all be back before dark. Maggie, you do exactly what Kelly tells you." She looked hard at her older daughter. "Where did you say you were going?"

"To the provincial park," Kelly answered quickly.

"That's all right. As long as you don't go onto the Indian Reserve. They don't want to be disturbed by summer people. And no lighting fires, do you understand?"

"But, Mum, I know how to do it properly—we learned at Guides," protested Kelly.

"This is a very dry summer. I don't want to take any chances. Give me your matches, Kelly." Aunt Ginnie held out her hand and Kelly dropped a book of matches into it.

Maggie was the first out the door. "Bye, Mummy! Bye, Rosemary!" she called jubilantly. Peggy jumped around her in circles, barking wildly.

Kelly paused when they reached the road. "Okay, let's go," she beckoned, leading them to the right.

"This isn't the way to the park!" objected Maggie. "Don't you even know where it is?"

Trevor groaned. "Shut up, Maggie, and don't ask questions."

"We're not going to the park," Kelly explained. "We're going to the Indian Reserve."

"But Mummy said—"

"I knew we shouldn't have brought her," said Christie impatiently.

Patricia listened to them reason with the little girl. It was handy having Maggie along to ask the questions she wasn't brave enough to ask herself.

"I know what Mum said," Kelly told her, "but she doesn't understand about the Indians. Last summer they said we could go on their land as long as we didn't litter. If you want to come with us you have to promise not to tell, okay?"

"Sure!" declared Maggie, proud to be included in a secret. "I won't tell. I bet Potty will, though."

"Will you?" asked Christie.

Patricia shook her head. She felt a twinge of superiority; she'd already been on the Indian Reserve today.

They trudged along the road. The heat had softened the tar and it stuck to Patricia's bare feet. She lifted them gingerly, trying not to mind; Ruth never wore shoes.

Past the last cottage was a group of dilapidated buildings labelled St. Stephen's Church Retreat.

"What's that?" asked Patricia. The shock of returning so abruptly from the past was wearing off; she felt *here* again.

"It used to be a camp," explained Kelly, "but it hasn't been used for years. We play in the cabins sometimes."

"Remember when Bruce found a kangaroo mouse in one?" said Christie.

Patricia shivered. It was too bad her cousins were so fond of toads and snakes and mice. She wondered if they had a test for her to pass today.

"I just wish we had some matches," grumbled Kelly.

"I have matches," said Bruce calmly.

Kelly's face lit up. "Great! Good for you, Bruce."

They reached a faded sign. Spruce Band Reserve it said. Speed Limit 30 MPH. Watch for Pedestrians, Livestock and Horse-Drawn Vehicles.

"That's really old," Bruce told Patricia. "The Indians don't use wagons anymore."

Kelly led them off the road onto a dirt path. Across it stretched a piece of barbed wire. Patricia's heart thudded as she scrambled under after the others.

Now they walked quietly. Maggie moved closer to Kelly and took her hand. Trevor tied a rope to Peggy's collar.

"Hi, Mr. Paul," called Kelly. She waved to an old man sitting on the steps of a bungalow.

"Hi, kids," the man said gravely. "You're back again."

"We're going to Sandy Point for a picnic. Is that all right?"

The man's brown face crinkled into a smile. "That's all right. Come back later. My grandsons will be home and you can have a ride."

"Thanks, we will!" said Kelly.

They continued past other small houses. Women eyed them curiously and small black-haired children stared. One teenaged boy with a long braid and fringed leather vest glared at them until they passed the houses.

"You're so brave, Kelly," whispered Christie. "I'm afraid to talk to them. Daddy would be furious if he knew we were here. He doesn't like the Indians, he says they're lazy."

Kelly stopped and faced her cousin. "I hope *you* don't think that, Christie Reid! They're people like you and me and white men have been horrible to them. Mr. Paul is my friend. You know we always rent horses from him. My parents say your father is prejudiced."

"He's not!" cried Christie and Bruce, but without much conviction.

"You know he is," said Kelly angrily. She continued walking, then added more kindly, "Never mind. You can't help what Uncle Rod's like, as long as you don't think the same way."

"We don't," Christie assured her, "but I'm still afraid of being here. It's their land, after all. We're trespassing."

"But you heard Mr. Paul say it was all right," said Kelly.

Patricia agreed with Christie about trespassing, but she didn't have the nerve to say so.

"Remember when *we* pretended we were Indians?" Trevor asked his sister. "You were Brave Eagle and I was Jumping Rabbit and Christie was Windrunner ..."

Kelly frowned. "We were a lot younger then."

"No, we weren't! Even last year ..."

Kelly's look stopped him. She glanced at Patricia and flushed.

She's embarrassed because of *me*! thought Patricia in wonder.

They reached the point and flopped down on the same sandy beach where Patricia had enjoyed her fish. For the next few hours the six of them swam, fished, made a fire and gorged themselves on the huge picnic Aunt Ginnie had packed. At first Patricia hung back, but the lake looked so inviting she surprised herself by joining a game of water tag. When Bruce offered to teach her how to fish she accepted gingerly; after all, Ruth could fish. She even caught a perch and impressed Kelly by knowing how to clean and cook it.

After supper she dozed in the sand, listening to the noisy crows and chickadees in the bushes behind her. Living in two different times was exhausting. Dreamily she reviewed the details of her morning in the past. She was still anxious about whether or not she could get back, but she wasn't in as much of a hurry. This afternoon had been unexpectedly pleasant; for the first time, her cousins didn't seem so threatening.

"Has anyone got any money?" Kelly asked after a lazy interlude. "I'm not sure I have enough to rent the horses."

"I do," said Trevor, emptying his pockets.

"Maggie, will you lend us some? You're always loaded." Kelly persuaded her sister to give up a dollar.

Patricia's calm mood vanished. Were they going to make her ride? Horses terrified her. Once her mother had persuaded her to take riding lessons, but Patricia couldn't get the old horse she was assigned to do anything and had begged not to go back. "I don't understand it," her mother had sighed. "When I was your age I longed to ride."

Kelly had finished counting the money. "There's enough for four of us to have a horse, as long as the rates are the same as last year."

"I don't mind not going," said Patricia quickly.

"It's all right," Christie assured her. "Maggie's too young and Bruce is allergic to horses. He can stay with her and Peggy while we're gone. Unless you're afraid," she added, a taunting edge returning to her voice.

"They're really gentle horses, Potty," said Kelly. "I promise you."

Was this a trick? Patricia didn't want to spoil the sense of belonging she was beginning to have. She decided to believe that the friendly tone of Kelly's voice was genuine. "Okay. As long as it's a slow one."

"Good!" said Kelly with an approving grin. She began to organize the packing and made sure the fire was completely out.

They reached Mr. Paul's house and went into an adjoining field. Patricia shivered as she gazed at the huge animal an Indian boy brought over to her. After the boy helped her up, the horse turned its head and glared at her with one unblinking eye. A strong horsey smell rose up around her. Her legs stuck out sideways on the broad back. There was no saddle and just a rope to hang onto.

Kelly laughed at her from the top of a smaller horse. "That's the fattest mare I've ever seen! You'll be lucky if you can even get her to walk."

Patricia hoped she was right. She was relieved when, despite banging her heels into the horse's sides, it lumbered far behind.

"Hurry up, Potty—get a switch!" they called.

But she couldn't reach a branch to use and she didn't want to hurt the horse. It seemed as reluctant as she was to go for a ride.

Christie trotted back and grabbed Patricia's horse's rope. "I'll have to lead you till we're out of sight of the field. She's just lazy. She'll go faster when she knows she can't go back."

It felt safer to have Christie attached to her, even though there was now only the mane to hang onto. Patricia laced her fingers firmly into the long stiff hairs.

Kelly led them up the road to the border of the Reserve. "We have time to go to the store and back," she suggested.

"But someone might see us!" said Christie.

"It's risky," admitted Kelly, "but wouldn't it be great if the Other Enders saw us? *They've* never had the guts to rent horses. Look, it's six o'clock. Mum was going to eat at your place—they'll all be down at the beach with the barbecue."

"The Other Enders could be eating, too," Trevor pointed out.

"Maybe … but they might have finished and be hanging around the store."

"I don't want to," said Christie. "It's taking too much of a chance. You know how angry Dad can get. He'd have a fit if he saw us on the Indians' horses."

But, as usual, Kelly had her way. They reached the road and formed a procession with Patricia between Christie and Trevor. Then her horse plodded reluctantly without being led.

Patricia began to relax a little but she still wished the ordeal was over. It didn't help to think of how Ruth would envy her. She just didn't like riding, that was all.

It seemed to take forever to reach the store. Kelly lingered hopefully in front of it but no one came out to admire them.

"Come on, Kelly, we should go back or we'll have to pay for another hour," said her brother.

Kelly turned her horse's head around and changed direction. Then all the horses began to trot.

"S-stop going so fast!" gasped Patricia. Her teeth clicked together at each jerky movement.

Christie looked back. "Don't worry. They just know they're going home, that's all. Sit as low as you can and grip the sides. That's the Western way of trotting— I learned it at riding lessons."

Patricia tried, but she was still being bounced high off the horse's back. It hurt. Then she tried posting, the way she remembered from her riding lessons, but that was impossible without any stirrups to rise up on. She pulled on the rope reins, but the horse was like a machine that she couldn't turn off.

"If we canter it'll be more comfortable," called Kelly. "Hi-*ya*!" She kicked her horse into a slow run. Patricia's horse eagerly copied the others. It was now easier to stay on, but Patricia was still terrified. The horse rocked rhythmically and grunted each time its hooves pounded the ground.

"Slow down!" she pleaded, pulling back on the rope as hard as she could. At least, at this pace, they would soon be there, but she'd much rather be walking. She gave another desperate jerk backwards.

The horse responded by lurching its head forward impatiently. Then it broke from the line and began to gallop.

Patricia screamed and threw herself forward onto the horse's neck. It charged full speed down the road. Bits of tar and grit flew into her eyes and mouth. With each pace she was flung inches into the air and slammed down hard.

I'll be killed, she thought dully as the trees rose and fell around her. She couldn't scream anymore and she knew that soon her arms would be too weak to clutch the animal's sweating neck.

A tall figure stepped into her path. "Whoa! Okay, I've got it!" The man grabbed the rope and pulled. The horse swung out to the side as it was jerked to a stop. Patricia slid off its back into the ditch.

Her mouth was full of dirt. She turned her head and wiped it out, staring up at a concerned face.

"Are you all right?" It was Mrs. Donaldson from next door. Her husband held the horse and tried to calm it down. The woman brushed off Patricia and stood her up.

Patricia cried uncontrollably. Sobs rose up from her belly and she started hiccuping. Mrs. Donaldson patted her on the back. "There, there, you're all right now. That must have been a nasty experience."

Her cousins cantered up and halted. Kelly scrambled off, handed her reins to Trevor and rushed over.

"Potty, are you all right? I've never known a horse to bolt so fast! You should have seen how high you bounced! Are you really all right?"

Patricia faced her cousin. "You s-said the horse was gentle!" she choked. "You p-promised!"

"They usually are! Honestly, Potty, I didn't know. There must be something wrong with it."

Patricia didn't believe her. Kelly had probably known all along that the horse was crazy—it was just another trick. She turned her back and let Mrs. Donaldson lead her to the cottage.

"AND YOU'RE NOT to use the canoe for a week. And no allowance for two weeks. And for the rest of today you're not to leave our property."

Patricia had never seen Aunt Ginnie like this. Her usually mild eyes blazed as she paced up and down in front of Kelly, Trevor, Maggie and Patricia, who were sitting in a row on the couch.

After Patricia had been brought in the night before, her aunt had hurried back from Uncle Rod's and fussed over her as if she were a baby. She gave Patricia a hot bath and put her to bed with an aspirin, trying to calm her shuddering sobs. Patricia had barely heard Kelly creep in beside her an hour later.

"Potty? Are you awake? Do you know why your horse ran away? It was pregnant! Mr. Paul was really mad at his grandsons for renting it to us. So it wasn't my fault, Potty. And I'm in trouble, too. Mum's so upset she won't speak to us, but I'll bet we'll get an earful tomorrow."

Patricia didn't answer. She kept her eyes tightly closed and tried to stop the bed from bouncing up and down like the horse.

This morning she was surprised to be included in Aunt Ginnie's scolding. "It's mostly Kelly and Trevor's fault, of course," her aunt said to her more gently, "but you knew you weren't supposed to go on the Reserve, Patricia, so I think it's fair that you be penalized as well."

"It's *not* fair, Mum!" protested Kelly. "She got the worst of it, bolting on that horse!"

Patricia frowned at her cousin. She didn't want her sympathy. "It's all right. I was wrong, too," she said quietly.

She couldn't remember ever being punished in her life; it was a novelty. Her parents didn't believe in punishment. A tiny part of her was even glad that she now belonged to the family enough to be treated equally.

Finally Aunt Ginnie's anger evaporated. She sighed, as if she were surprised it had surfaced at all. "All right, that's all I have to say. But I don't know what your father will think when he arrives. Now all of you go and do something quiet."

It was a cool, rainy Saturday morning with no swimming lessons to attend. The others sat on the verandah glumly, shuffling a pack of cards. Patricia edged away from them.

"Do you want to play poker with us?" Kelly asked her.

"No thanks—I want to be alone," Patricia walked through the rain to La Petite and lay stiffly on the bed for a few minutes, warming the watch in her hands.

She was sore all over from the terrible ride. And she ached inside, too. The trust she had begun to feel at the picnic was shattered. Kelly knew everything. She should have known there was something wrong with the horse. Whether or not it was a deliberate trick, it was Kelly's fault that it had happened.

Never had she wanted to escape to the past so much. She decided to wind the watch as far as it would go and stay longer.

But would the knob still be stuck? Patricia sat up and tried it with sweating hands.

It moved easily. She worked it between her thumb and forefinger until she felt a resistance. Then she closed her eyes.

10

*P*atricia was prepared to begin her time in the past in the same place where she had wound the watch, so she was not surprised to open her eyes in La Petite. Now she noticed how new the cabin was: the floorboards had the tart smell of freshly cut lumber.

She remembered that she'd left Ruth and Ginnie walking up the path from the Main Beach and ran out to meet them. Ruth was red with exertion from lugging Ginnie on her back. "I'm sure your toe's better by now," she said crossly.

The little girl looked tragic. "No, it's not, Ruthie! I think it's broken!"

Patricia followed them into the cottage with delight. She was safe again. Now she could forget about runaway horses and broken promises. It was too painful to trust people. Here, no one could hurt her.

The watch, fully wound, lasted for two days. Once Patricia tried the knob, but it wouldn't move. For some reason the watch could only be wound in the present, as if it weren't real in the past. On the afternoon of the first day, Patricia discovered something that confirmed this.

She was perched on a stool in Ruth's parents' bedroom, watching Pat Reid put her older daughter's hair up in pincurls. Ginnie squatted on the floor and made a long chain of bobby pins. Ruth sat in a low chair while her mother worked around her head, coiling wet ropes of hair and securing each fat circle with two crossed pins. It seemed like a lot of work.

Ruth twisted her head impatiently. "I wish I could get my hair cut. This takes so long."

"Long hair is more suitable for a girl your age," mumbled her mother through the bobby pins that she held between her lips. "I don't enjoy this any more than you do, Ruth. It's about time you learned to do it yourself."

"I've tried," complained Ruth, "but the hair keeps unwinding before I can get it fastened." She was beginning to look as if she were wearing a metal cap. "Mother," she continued, "am I old enough to go out with a boy?"

Her mother removed the pins from her mouth and stared sternly at her daughter. "Definitely not. You're only twelve."

"I didn't say I was going to. I just wanted to know if I was old enough."

"Did someone ask you?"

Ruth looked embarrassed. "Ummm … yes. To the costume party at the rec hall."

Her mother went back to making pincurls. "I heard about that yesterday. The whole beach will be there. Your father will have to bring something from the city for us to dress up in. But you'll go with the rest of the family, not alone with a boy. Who asked you?"

"Just Tom Turner. But I said no. I don't *want* to go with him; he's a show-off like Rodney."

"I certainly hope you don't. You're much too young." There was a long pause. "You're an attractive girl, you know. In fact, your Aunt Sophie admitted to me you were the prettiest in the family—certainly prettier than her two." She and Ruth examined Ruth's reflection as if it belonged to someone else.

"You're one of the lucky ones," her mother sighed. "But good looks are a responsibility. Boys are going to start paying attention to you too soon. You just make sure you remind them how old you are."

Ruth looked bewildered. "But why is it so important? I didn't choose to look any particular way."

"None of us did, did we?" said her mother dryly. "But looks *are* important—for a girl they're all that matters."

"Am *I* 'tractive, Mama?" asked Ginnie from the floor.

Her mother laughed. "You're Mama's beautiful dumpling, sweetheart. Undo all those pins now, I need them."

"Where's your watch, Mama?" asked Ginnie as she climbed onto the bed and began to unhook the bobby pins. "Why aren't you wearing it? I want to hear it tick."

"You know I don't wear my watch at the lake. It might get damaged. I've put it away for the summer in my jewellery case."

"Can I look at it?" Ginnie was already lifting the lid of a wooden box on the dresser.

"If you're careful."

Patricia began to tremble. She clutched the watch around her neck. What would Pat Reid say when she discovered it was missing? And how had the watch got from the jewelry case to La Petite? She felt as guilty as if she had stolen it.

Then Ginnie pulled a long chain from the box and dangled a gold watch in the air. "Here it is!"

No! thought Patricia. It can't be—I'm wearing it around my neck.

But the watch looked exactly like hers. Shinier, perhaps, but with the same black numerals and the same glass insert. Patricia knew it was the same one. Impossibly, it was both lying unwound in Ginnie's palm and ticking away the seconds on her chest. Just as she really didn't belong here, her watch didn't either. It was as if they were both ghosts—ghosts from the future.

Ginnie pressed the knob on the watch she held. "Look, I made it open!"

"Be careful, you'll break it," her mother mumbled through bobby pins. "Close it for her, Ruth."

Ruth took the watch from her sister but before she snapped it shut she studied the inscription. "Is 1929 the year Father's brother died?"

"Yes … he died the week before our wedding date. The watch was an engagement present." She crossed the last two pins on Ruth's head, reached for the watch and caressed its chain.

"What was he like?" prompted Ruth, but her mother's expression was distant and she didn't seem to hear.

Ginnie scrambled onto the bed. "Can I wind it up?"

Pat Reid stood up abruptly and put the watch back. "No, Ginnie—I've let it run down. Now go out into the sun, you two. I want to finish my book."

PATRICIA SLEPT BESIDE Ruth that night, lying on top of the covers in the same position next to the wall that she occupied in the bed with Kelly. She awoke refreshed, overjoyed that she was still in the past.

That morning Andrew Reid drove the boys and Ruth—and Patricia—into town. Patricia hadn't been there yet, although she knew it was where the power plant was located in the present. Today the town was a peaceful-looking collection of ramshackle wooden buildings. Hardly anyone was in the streets and the woman in the tiny post office looked up sleepily when the Reids pushed through the door to collect the mail.

Andrew Reid frowned at the letter he had opened. "It's a good thing I'm going back to the city on Monday. They can't seem to run the law firm properly without me."

"Will you bring us some new badminton birds next weekend, sir?" Rodney asked him as they walked to the general store.

"And I need a polishing cloth for my telescope—I'll write down the brand," added Gordon. The boys and their father strode confidently down the street, Ruth lingering behind.

Patricia paused with her when she stopped to stroke a horse that was tethered to a wagon in front of the store.

The back of the wagon was full of Indian children, their dark eyes watching Ruth cautiously.

"You like horses?" the biggest boy asked.

Ruth nodded, her face buried in the horse's neck. Patricia was careful not to get too near, even though the horse couldn't hurt her when she was invisible.

"Ruth! Get away from there!" Andrew Reid's deep voice broke the torpid silence of the street as he and the boys came out of the store loaded with groceries.

Ruth joined them reluctantly. Her father didn't say anything to her until they were back at the grey car. Then he put down his bag and turned her around by the shoulders to face him.

"Listen to me, young lady. You are not to speak to the Indians! I've told you that before. We mind our business and they mind theirs. Your mother would be furious if she knew you'd been near those children—they didn't look very clean."

"I was just patting the horse ..." Ruth began, but her father's fierce expression quelled her.

All the way back to the cottage Patricia studied the back of Andrew Reid's neck. It bristled with short white hairs and was as stiff and immobile as a tree trunk. She couldn't help thinking about Wilfred. He may have been Andrew's brother, but she was sure he must have been nicer.

AT THE DINNER TABLE that night Andrew Reid gave his children a General Knowledge quiz. Even Ginnie had a turn.

"All right, Ginnie. Who's the most famous skater in Canada?"

"Barbara Ann Scott!" she crowed. "I want a Barbara Ann Scott doll for my birthday, Papa."

"How many provinces are there?" her father asked the older children.

"Nine," said Rodney.

Ruth looked smug. "You're wrong, Rodney. Newfoundland just joined."

"Good for you, Ruth," her father said grudgingly. "You should have known that," he told his sons.

When Ruth answered more questions correctly, he was even sterner. "Are you going to let a girl beat you, boys? You'd better start reading the paper."

A few hours later the family went down to the beach for a bonfire. Ginnie lay wrapped in a blanket on her mother's lap, her eyes closing and opening as she struggled to stay awake. Ruth roasted a marshmallow an even brown as her father and the boys adjusted Gordon's telescope. Then they played word games until it got dark.

Patricia lay on her back on the pebbly beach and stared with wonder at the countless stars above her. She had never seen this many except in a planetarium.

Gordon peered through his telescope with his head cocked sideways. "I think I've got Jupiter. Look, Rodney, you can see its moons." The telescope, which looked homemade, was a large black tube mounted on a wooden stand.

Everyone except Ruth's mother took a turn gazing through it. "I can't see anything through that contraption," she complained. "I'd rather use my eyes. Tell us some of the constellations, Gordon."

They all lay down, even Andrew Reid, who looked undignified spread full length on the beach. Gordon's voice was eager as he pointed out stars. "There's Scorpius—see that reddish star? That's Antares, the largest star in the sky."

Patricia tried to trace the scorpion's tail. For a few seconds it stood out until she blinked. She found the patterns of Lyra and Sagittarius more easily.

They sat up and the boys peered through the telescope again. Ginnie had given in to sleep. Ruth's back was towards her family her arms clasped around her knees as she gazed at the black lake. The water lapped softly and a loon warbled.

Andrew Reid pulled on his pipe and blew out a swirl of bitter-smelling smoke. "We're a lucky family, Pat," he said gruffly. "Four healthy children and a place like this to come to."

His wife was staring into the fire. "Yes, Andrew," she said distantly. Then she sighed and turned to him as if she had just heard his words. "Yes, we are lucky. Thank goodness the boys were too young for the war and you were too old."

"It's a wonderful time to be young," her husband continued. "I envy you boys. The world's at peace.

Edmonton will boom with that oil discovery in Leduc. You should both be able to make successes of yourselves."

Ruth turned around. "What about me?"

"Why, I want you and Ginnie to marry well and raise large families. I want lots of grandchildren!" her father smiled.

"What if I don't have children?"

"Don't be silly, Ruth—of course you will," her mother said. Patricia reminded herself that Ruth would grow up to be her mother. She shivered, feeling more like a ghost than ever.

"I HAVE A TREAT FOR US," said Pat Reid the next morning. "Kay Weber's brother is an Anglican clergyman, and he's here for the weekend. He's going to conduct a service at their cottage tomorrow morning. You know how much I miss church at the lake."

"Church in the summer, Ma! That's too much," groaned Gordon.

"I'll pass, thank you," said Rodney.

"Me, too," added Ruth.

Ginnie pouted. "I hate going to church, Mama, it's so boring."

Even her husband looked resentful, although he didn't say anything.

Pat Reid stared at them, the anger rising in her face like water filling a glass. She clapped her palms on the table. "You will *all* go, with no rude remarks or complaints. All of you! If we can't go to church together ..." Her voice grew shriller with each word.

Andrew Reid shot a warning glance at his children, then spoke calmly. "All right, Pat. Of course we'll go. Apologize to your mother at once, children."

There was a mumbled chorus of "sorrys." Everyone's breath was stilled while they waited to see if Pat Reid's outburst would subside. Her voice became steadier.

"Very well. Tomorrow morning at ten o'clock."

RIGHT AFTER they got back from the church service the next morning, the watch ran out. Ruth was again sitting on the Main Beach with Ginnie, reading to her from a book called *Just Mary*. Patricia found herself back in the present right in the middle of a sentence. Then she lay on the bed in La Petite for a long time.

She was worn out. It was too much, darting back and forth in time. This trip had been such a long one, she didn't know if she could go through another extended period yet, even though she much preferred being there than here.

She hid the watch and strolled out into the rain, blinking as she tried to become accustomed to being back. For the rest of the day she joined Kelly and the others, still grounded, on the verandah. They didn't seem to mind her being with them; Kelly even looked relieved that she'd returned. But Patricia wouldn't give in to her friendly overtures. For the first time, she felt superior to Kelly. Her cousin knew how to do a lot of things Patricia didn't, but she didn't know Patricia's secret.

Uncle Doug arrived for the weekend and they had to listen to another lecture about the horses. At least it didn't last long; he wasn't as good at scolding as his wife.

He'd brought Patricia a letter from her mother. It was her usual short account of current events, written with forced cheerfulness. All about her work and nothing about the separation. Patricia shuddered at the strangeness of reading a letter from Ruth at age forty-seven when she'd just been sitting beside her on the beach at age twelve. The two Ruths were so different. What had happened to turn the girl she liked so much into her mother?

That evening Patricia had disturbing news. "Your Nan's coming, dear," beamed Aunt Ginnie. "She phoned this afternoon. She's very excited—she hasn't seen you since you were eight!"

For a few seconds Patricia was indifferent. She wrote to her grandmother in Calgary twice a year, thanking her for birthday and Christmas cheques. She could hardly remember what she looked like.

Then she put down the piece of watermelon she was eating as she realized with shock what Aunt Ginnie had said. Nan was Pat Reid. The woman Patricia had been watching in the past was coming *here*.

And Patricia had her watch. Surely Nan didn't know it had been under the floor in the cabin. She must have lost it long ago. Patricia didn't want to give it back; it felt like her watch now.

She asked shakily, "When is Nan coming?"

"Around noon on Tuesday. Uncle Doug's taking the day off to drive her out. She'll stay in La Petite. You and Kelly can help me tidy it up."

"Don't forget I'm doing the floor tomorrow," Uncle Doug reminded her.

Now Patricia was frantic. What if they found the watch under the mattress? She would have to look for a new hiding place.

She finished her dessert with difficulty. She didn't want to meet her grandmother as she was now; the past and the present would get all mixed up.

11

*W*hen Nan arrived, Patricia hid behind the others so she could observe her privately, the way she did when she was invisible.

A thin figure stepped carefully out of the car. She was very different from the woman Patricia knew from thirty-five years ago. Shorter, with her back and shoulders curving into a stoop. Instead of a cotton dress, she wore green pants and a loose top that looked out of place with the double strand of pearls knotted around her wiry neck. Her hair was permed into even, iron-grey curls. Although her ugly mouth still twisted when it smiled, her expression had become aggressive instead of vague.

The biggest difference was that she gushed. "My darling children … give your old Nan a kiss!" she cried in a sugary voice. "Here's the baby, what a sweetheart— hand her to me. Hello, Ginnie, dear, how lovely to be here! And Maggie … and my own Trevor."

Patricia listened in wonder. Maybe her grandmother had grown more affectionate after her husband died. But there was something forced and smothering about her cooing. As everyone was embraced again and again, Patricia hid behind the car.

"But where's Patricia?" the strident voice cried. "Where's my poor little Patricia?"

Aunt Ginnie put an encouraging arm around her niece. "Don't be shy, dear. Come and say hello to your grandmother."

Nan gave Rosemary back to Aunt Ginnie and took Patricia's face in her hands. Patricia jerked her head with embarrassment, but the cool palms held it firmly.

"So this is Patricia … finally!" Nan kissed her quickly and released her hold. "You don't look at all like your mother. Well, perhaps that's just as well. Do you know I haven't seen you for four years? We'll have to have a good long talk."

Patricia escaped by helping to carry suitcases into La Petite. Her stomach churned with guilt as she glanced at the bed and the newly tiled floor. Early Sunday morning she had crept into the cabin and rescued the watch. She'd hidden it up in the attic of the cottage, concealed in an empty shoebox she'd found in a corner. No one ever went up there; it was far too hot.

"A good long talk": the ominous words rang in her ears all day. She began to relax, though, when she saw that there were too many people around for Nan to get her alone. Uncle Rod's family arrived and Patricia was protected from her grandmother by a thicket of chatter.

Everyone waited on the old woman. Aunt Ginnie and Aunt Karen hovered around her, keeping her supplied with cigarettes, tea and cushions. Nan was much bossier and more opinionated than in the past.

Before dinner she shooed the women into the kitchen and sat on the verandah with Uncle Rod, having a lively argument with him about the prime minister. Trevor, Christie and Bruce crouched at her feet. Kelly had disappeared somewhere.

Patricia sat on the front steps, holding the baby. She watched Uncle Doug tend the barbecue and Maggie practise handstands on the lawn.

Rosemary babbled and snatched at Patricia's nose and hair. Patricia bounced her, whispering a rhyme she'd heard her aunt use:

> *This is the way*
> *The ladies ride*
> *Nim, nim, nim …*

Uncle Doug and Maggie came up the steps. "Do you want me to take the baby?" offered her uncle.

"It's okay," said Patricia. It calmed her to hold the plump little body. Besides, it gave her an excuse not to join the noisy group inside. Rosemary was heavy however, and after a while Patricia placed her carefully on the grass.

Kelly appeared and joined her on the steps. Patricia wriggled nervously. "Do you think the ground is too damp for her?" she asked, pointing to the baby to draw attention away from herself.

"Oh, no—babies are tough. Come here, Piglet. Now, watch this …" Kelly lugged her sister to her lap, then gently lifted her by the ankles until she hung upside-down.

"Don't!" cried Patricia. "You'll hurt her!"

Kelly laughed. "No, I won't. She loves it."

And, sure enough, Rosemary arched her back and smiled at this new view of the world. All the same Patricia was relieved when Kelly put her back on the grass.

A chipmunk scuttled across the lawn. Behind them, the buzz of talk rose and fell.

"So what do you think of Nan?" Kelly asked.

"Oh. She's ... fine, I guess. I haven't really talked to her."

"Maybe you'll get to be one of her pets, like Trevor. He's her favourite. She doesn't care for me much." Kelly's voice was matter-of-fact.

"Why not?" Patricia couldn't help asking.

"Because I'm 'wild' and 'a tomboy' and 'don't dress properly.'" Her cousin imitated her grandmother's tone so perfectly that Patricia smiled in spite of herself.

"She lives in a fancy condominium in Calgary," Kelly continued, "and whenever we go there, I have to wear a dress and pass tea to old ladies or help arrange flowers in the church. It's incredibly old-fashioned. Christie likes it, but she's strange sometimes. Everyone thinks Nan is so sweet—but she isn't always. Once I accidentally broke an old dish and she really blew her top. It was weird, as if she'd turned into another person. I thought she was going to hit me. She said something queer then ... she said I reminded her of Ruth."

Patricia started. "Of wh-who?"

"Ruth. Your mother, silly. Mum says I look a bit like she did at my age. Bet I won't be as gorgeous, though. But who would want to be? Does she like getting all made up and looking so glamorous all the time?"

Patricia stiffened. "How would *I* know?"

"Well, she *is* your mother. Honestly, Potty, sometimes you get so touchy." Offended, Kelly turned from Patricia to the baby.

Rosemary had hoisted herself to her side and was lying there like a beached seal. Then, with a flop, she landed on her stomach. She grinned with surprise.

"You turned over, Piglet—good for you!" Picking up the baby, Kelly rushed inside to tell her mother.

FOR THE NEXT two days, Patricia managed to avoid being alone with Nan. Her grandmother gave her an appraising, quizzical glance from time to time, but there were no more suggestions of a talk. Patricia hoped she had forgotten about it.

She longed for the watch and wished she could slip up to the attic and escape to the past. But it was impossible to be alone this week. Nan came to the beach with them every morning and sat under an umbrella while they had their swimming lessons. The two fathers had returned to the city, and every afternoon the mothers took Nan and the cousins on a different excursion. They drove to the Pembina river valley to pick wild strawberries, formed a fishing fleet of two canoes and a rowboat and visited friends on the other side of the lake. Every night they all ate together, Nan presiding like a queen.

Sometimes she and Aunt Ginnie told stories of past summers at the lake. Patricia shivered with the strangeness of it when they mentioned something she knew, such as how Aunt Ginnie was so frightened of going to the outhouse at night that one of her parents had to go with her and talk reassuringly outside the door.

"You were a spoiled one," laughed Nan fondly. She never mentioned Ruth in her stories.

Once she showed her grandchildren her scrapbook of the Royal Family. "I have twenty-two of them," she said proudly. "One day they'll be valuable. Look, Maggie, here's little Prince William with his parents."

"His dad sure has huge ears," commented Maggie.

Uncle Doug and Uncle Rod arrived and departed with the weekend. By Monday, Aunt Ginnie had run out of ideas for outings and Kelly especially was itching to be on her own.

"Let's see …" mused her mother after lunch. "What would you like to do, Mama? We could walk down to the other end and visit old Mrs. Thorpe."

"Mum," interrupted Kelly, "can we go and finish our fort? We haven't been near it for a week."

"I'd like you to come with us to the Thorpes, Kelly. You never see their children—you shouldn't stick to yourselves so much."

Kelly made a rude face.

"Oh, let them go off and play, Ginnie," said Nan. "I've monopolized them so far. I can visit Muriel

Thorpe this evening. Right now I'd like to have some time with Patricia. Shall we go out to La Petite and have a nice chat? I'm sure you'd like to be left alone as well, Ginnie."

Everyone but Patricia looked grateful. She lingered in the driveway as her grandmother walked towards La Petite with quick steps, but finally she had to follow her into the cabin.

Nan plugged in the electric kettle and set out tea supplies on a small table. "I'm beginning to have enough of roughing it," she frowned, examining a chipped mug. "Soon you'll have to come and visit me in Calgary and I'll show you the Coalport china your great-grandmother left me."

Patricia didn't answer. She sat tensely on the edge of one of the beds worrying about the watch. She was sure that, somehow, Nan was going to mention it.

But it wasn't the watch Nan wanted to talk about. Afterwards Patricia thought how foolish she'd been to imagine that it would be. Nan had no reason to connect the watch with her granddaughter.

She began by recalling the last time she'd seen Patricia. "You were so plump," she laughed. "Just like Ginnie at that age. I don't know how your mother could leave you with a babysitter."

"But she was nice," protested Patricia softly. Hannah had looked after her all day until she went to kindergarten, and after school later on. She'd told her stories and let her help make cookies.

"Nice or not, I don't agree with this modern notion of mothers working. I told your parents so and unfortunately we had such a great argument about it that I didn't visit again. And every time I've asked Ruth to let you come to me, she's put me off. Photographs are all very well, but they're no substitute. But now I have you in person at last. I'd like the two of us to become friends, Patricia. Your mother and I have always clashed. But you and I can begin again."

If being friends meant her grandmother talking to her as if she were an adult, Patricia wanted no part of it. She didn't want to hear about past arguments. But then her grandmother went much further.

"Now, I want to hear *your* version of this sad business with your parents," she pronounced, handing Patricia a mug of tea. "Ruth won't tell me, of course. But you can. I've always approved of your father—he's a sensible, decent man. What did she do to drive him away? Too headstrong as usual, I suspect."

Patricia was so stunned, she didn't even notice the mug was burning her hand. Nan's voice had an almost satisfied ring to it, as if she had known all along that Ruth's marriage would fail. She began to grill Patricia, who barely whispered her replies.

"Is there a specific reason they're separating?"

"I don't know."

"Is your mother seeing another man?"

"I don't know."

"What about your father? Is he seeing someone else?"

Patricia revived a little; this was nobody's business. "I *don't know*," she said more loudly.

Nan sighed. "Oh, Patricia." Her voice softened. "I'm not trying to pry—I have to ask you because Ruth will never tell me."

Patricia set her untasted tea on the table. She was freezing cold and there was a painful cramp in her stomach. "I have to leave," she muttered. "I don't feel well."

Nan became a charming grandmother again. "Of course, poor darling. Is it your tummy?"

Patricia nodded and pushed out of La Petite. She ran to the cottage, dashed into the bathroom and sat on the toilet for a long time. Then she spent the rest of the afternoon shivering under the heavy quilt on Kelly's bed.

A KNOCK ON THE DOOR woke her from a jangled dream.

"Patricia?" called Aunt Ginnie in a concerned voice. "Do you feel better? Do you want to get up and try eating something?"

Patricia got out of bed groggily. She felt nothing at all, as if her body had disappeared—the way it did in the past.

At least Nan was out for dinner at the Thorpes. Patricia went through the motions of eating, then played checkers with Maggie in a dazed stupor.

"I won again!" crowed Maggie. "You're not very good at this, are you, Potty. Want to play for money?"

Patricia heard Nan coming up the back steps and hung her head over the checkerboard.

"Hello, my darlings," said the syrupy voice. "Having a nice, cosy evening? And Patricia, are you better?"

Patricia nodded, but then wished she'd thought of saying no so she could go back to bed.

Aunt Ginnie carried in cocoa as Kelly and Trevor burst through the door, out of breath and giggling.

"What's green, red and yellow and rides up and down?" Trevor asked his grandmother.

"I have no idea, pet."

"A pickle, a tomato and a banana in an elevator."

The laughing group settled around the fire. Patricia stroked Peggy's head for comfort. Once again, everyone was feeling cheerful except herself.

"You remind me of Wilfred with your fooling, Trevor," said Nan. "He loved practical jokes. Once he disguised his voice and telephoned our house to apply for a job as a maid. Mother was completely taken in, until he told her he had to be paid in cigars!"

"Who's Wilfred?" Maggie asked her. "Do I know him?"

Once again, Patricia heard about Wilfred. Over the years, however, the story had become elaborated: Wilfred had died the very day of the wedding. Nan's voice gloated over the details as if the memory were an aching tooth she kept prodding. Even through her misery, Patricia couldn't help feeling a glimmer of pity for the sentimental, disappointed old woman.

Kelly yawned obviously and Aunt Ginnie looked worried. "Now, Mama, that's enough about Wilfred. What's past is past …" She nodded knowingly towards the children.

But Nan couldn't seem to stop. She began to tell Maggie, the only one who was really listening, about the watch Wilfred had given her. Patricia had been dozing, curled up against the warm dog. Now her stomach lurched again.

"It was a Half Hunter," said Nan dreamily. "It had a glass window so you could read the hands without opening it and it was fourteen carat gold. But it was lost years ago."

"How did it get lost?" asked Maggie.

"Through my own carelessness ..." Her voice drifted to a stop.

Trevor put a new log on the fire and it spat and popped as it flared up. Outside on the lake a loon cried faintly. Patricia shuddered. She could change that sad look on Nan's face—if she gave her back the watch.

"If you had married that guy, Nan," said Trevor brightly, "none of us would be here! You wouldn't have had Uncle Rod and Aunt Ruth and Mum—we wouldn't even exist!"

"And what a shame that would have been," said Nan. "No Trevor to tell me jokes, just imagine. But I married your grandfather."

"You would rather have married Wilfred, though." Kelly's honest blue eyes looked calmly at her grandmother.

"Kelly!" admonished her mother.

Patricia steeled herself for Nan's reaction. But Nan's answer was mild. "Wilfred *was* my first love, Kelly, but your grandfather and I had a good life together. Despite the difference in our ages, we made our marriage work. Which is more than I can say for Ruth," she sniffed.

Patricia flinched and sat upright.

"Mama ..." warned Aunt Ginnie, but at the same time Kelly asked, "What do you mean?"

"I mean Patricia's mother. Marriage is a lifelong commitment and—"

"Mama!" Aunt Ginnie leaned forward and shook her mother's shoulder. "That is a topic we will not discuss!"

It was too late. Kelly and Trevor turned to Patricia with surprised, fascinated faces.

Patricia jumped up and faced her grandmother. Anger flooded her like water from an unplugged dam. She choked with its force and struggled to turn it into words.

"I—I *hate* you!" she burst out finally. She ran into Kelly's bedroom and slammed the door.

WHEN KELLY JOINED her an hour later she lay beside Patricia quietly for a few minutes. Then she whispered, "Don't worry, Potty, we'll keep it a secret. Mum made us promise not to talk about it."

Her voice was kind, but Patricia was tired of promises. Her anger had released a kind of cold power inside; it was easy to direct it upon Kelly and she refused to answer.

After her cousin fell asleep she began to plan. She had to get back to the past as soon as possible, where no one knew about her or her parents, where she could be invisible. But she couldn't go until after Nan left on Wednesday.

Then she almost laughed out loud. She'd thought she didn't have enough time to be by herself this week, but she'd forgotten that, while she was in the past, no time passed in the present. She could go now! All she needed were the few seconds it took to wind the watch.

But today had been so harrowing. She was too drained to creep up to the attic and get the watch. Tomorrow morning would do. Then she would go back for a long time. Maybe she would just keep winding up the watch and stay forever.

*T*he next morning Aunt Ginnie called Patricia into her bedroom when she was dressed. "Your Nan didn't realize what she was saying last night. Lately she's been rambling more and more and I worry about her." She sighed. "It's hard to accept it when people grow old."

At breakfast the other children passed her the cereal before she asked for it and let her have the prize inside. Then Nan took her aside and apologized. "I got carried away, darling. Your mother has always had that effect on me. And I wasn't aware Ginnie hadn't told the others. Will you forgive your old Nan?"

I will never forgive you, thought Patricia. She ducked to avoid Nan's kiss but it caught her on the side of her head.

"I don't feel like going swimming," Patricia told Aunt Ginnie in a tight voice. "Is it all right if I stay here?"

"Of course, dear." Aunt Ginnie gave her a look of such loving concern that Patricia almost shouted, "Leave me alone!"

A little later, when she *was* alone, she savoured her solitude for a few minutes. She had never been in the cottage by herself, either in the past or in the present. The small house, layered with the accumulations of generations, fitted comfortably into either time. Patricia rocked in the creaking wicker chair, staring at Maggie's colouring book lying on the rug, its pages held open by Ginnie's wooden crayon box. It wouldn't have surprised her if both Ruth and Kelly had come into the room together.

But she knew she had to wind up the watch to really get back to the past. She shook herself alert and climbed the stairs to the attic.

A cloud of stale air engulfed her. Her nose tickled with dust as she picked up the shoebox and took out the watch. With much difficulty she pushed up a stiff window and squatted on the floor beside it, gulping in the fresh breeze.

For a few seconds she gazed reverently at the watch. It was miraculous that a portion of the past was contained in a golden disk she could hold in her hand. A handful of time. A time that somehow claimed her more than her own. How lucky she was to have found the watch exactly when she needed it. But how had it become lost? She wished she could solve its mystery.

She twisted the knob, listened to the reassuring metallic tick, then hung the watch around her neck. She turned her head. Now there were two unmade beds in the attic. Boys' shirts and socks littered the floor. She wondered how Gordon and Rodney could bear to sleep in such a stuffy room.

At first Patricia couldn't remember where the watch had left her last time. Then she recalled sitting on the beach while Ruth read to Ginnie. They would still be there, about to return to lunch. Footsteps moved around the kitchen below. She crept down the stairs and found Ruth's mother making sandwiches.

She was slicing bread efficiently. Patricia watched her with distaste, amazed at her own stupidity. She had tried to escape Nan by leaving her in the present. But she had forgotten—how could she?—that Nan was also part of the past. Usually she was able to cast off her own time and worries as soon as she wound the watch. Now her much younger grandmother's piercing eyes reminded her painfully of them.

But at least, in this time, Nan wasn't aware of Patricia. Here she couldn't question or embarrass her. She didn't even know her granddaughter existed.

Patricia stuck her tongue out at her. Then she went out to the front steps to wait for Ruth.

To MAKE SURE that she would stay in the past for as long a time as possible, Patricia wound the watch so that it would last for two days, and then rewound it as quickly as possible whenever it ran down and took her back to the attic. She soon became used to these brief flashes to the present—like turning over in her sleep and opening her eyes for an instant.

One evening after dinner she was surprised to hear Rodney mention that the family had been at the lake for only a week. "It's great that we still have almost two months until school starts," he said to Gordon. They were cleaning the telescope on the verandah. Ruth was bent over her puzzle.

Patricia did a rapid calculation and realized he was right. Only a week had passed here since she had first seen them playing badminton and arguing. It had been longer than that in her own time because of all the days during Nan's visit when she hadn't come.

"Is everything ready for tonight?" Rodney whispered to Gordon.

Ruth looked up suspiciously. "What's happening? What are you doing tonight?"

"Nothing's happening, infant," said Gordon. "Run away and leave us alone. Shouldn't you be helping Ma with the dishes?"

"They're done. I have as much right to be here as you have." Ruth's brothers just grinned, sharing a secret.

That night Ruth slept in her clothes. She kept the curtains open and seemed to be listening for something.

Patricia yawned. She wished they could go to sleep. In the morning she had swum a lot; she was beginning to relish the biting water that was colder and cleaner than it was in the present.

But Ruth continued to bob restlessly, looking out the window. Then she listened especially hard, pushed the window up high, lowered it again onto the top notch of the piece of wood that held it open, and squirmed out.

Patricia followed her reluctantly. She was not much of a climber and it was tricky to copy the way Ruth swung herself into a tree and slithered down. But she didn't want to miss anything and, soon, hurrying to keep up with Ruth's rapid trot, she was wide awake with curiosity.

The stars blazed overhead and Patricia kept her head up in wonder as she ran along the road. They were going in the direction of the Indian Reserve.

Soon they heard muffled laughter. Ahead of them was a group of teenagers: Gordon and Rodney, two other boys and two girls.

"I caught you!" Ruth called triumphantly.

Patricia watched Rodney's startled face with satisfaction. "What are you doing here?" he said angrily. Gordon glowered at his sister.

"I could ask *you* that," said Ruth. She tucked her hands into her pockets and looked up calmly at the six figures surrounding her. "You're going to raid the camp, aren't you?"

"You get home right now, Ruth," ordered Gordon.

"You can't make me. I want to come, too. If you don't let me, I'll tell."

"Looks like you don't have a choice, Reid," said one of the boys. His red hair matched the girls'—he must be their brother. Patricia recognized them from the store: they were the Thorpes, the ones who'd asked Rodney to the marshmallow roast.

"Let her come," said the other boy. It was Tom Turner. "She's pretty gutsy following us."

Her brothers refused to speak to her, but the girls were friendly as they continued along the shadowy road. "This is spooky!" one of them shivered. "Are you scared, Ruth?"

Ruth shook her head. They reached a sign that Patricia had seen before: St. Stephen's Church Retreat.

But now it was freshly painted and the long cabins beyond it looked new.

"What do we do now?" giggled the girl they called Barbara.

"We'll just give the kids a scare," said Gordon. "You and Winnie and Ruth come with me. Paul and Tom and Rodney can take care of the cabin on the other side. When I hoot twice like an owl, Paul, that will be the signal. Rodney has everything you need. Then run! We'll meet back at the Owens' pier."

"But what if they catch us?" asked Winnie.

"They never have. Everything's so dark, even the councillors must be asleep. By the time they wake up properly we'll be gone."

Even though no one could catch *her*, Patricia was glad she was with Gordon as their group crept through the trees to the nearest cabin. She felt as excited as Ruth looked.

Gordon halted the three girls and instructed them in an authoritative voice. He likes bossing people, thought Patricia, but he's good at it. Rodney likes it, too, but he's not.

"After I hoot," whispered Gordon, "start making spooky noises and throw these through the window. Then follow me as fast as you can."

He handed out knotted plastic bags filled with water. Then the four figures sneaked up to the glassless windows. Patricia peered in and saw a dozen sleeping bodies rolled in blankets. She waited tensely for Gordon's signal.

"Hoo-hoo-hoooooo ..." and then the same call again.

The girls began to moan. "Whoooooooo ..." Four assorted ghostly voices floated on the night air and four arms flung water bombs into the cabin. A fifth voice made the spookiest noises, but no one heard. Patricia was enjoying herself. After all, she was more like a ghost than any of them.

Shrieks and thumps came from inside. An older male voice shouted, "Who's there? Stop!"

But now Patricia was flying down the road with the others. Her hair whipped backwards and she laughed with exhilaration. Never before had she done something mischievous on purpose. It felt deliciously wicked.

The shouting voice followed them, but it faded as they cut through the bushes and stumbled along the stony beach to the Owens' cottage. It wasn't until they collapsed on the pier that Patricia noticed one person was missing.

"Ruth's gone!" she cried, but of course they couldn't hear her. Rodney, Tom and Paul arrived seconds later. Everyone whispered at once; no one commented on Ruth's absence.

It's as if she doesn't exist! thought Patricia angrily. As if she were invisible, like me.

Finally Tom said, "Hey, Reid, where's your sister?"

They all looked around. "Oh, no!" groaned Rodney. "I knew we shouldn't have let her come."

"She's a pest," agreed Gordon. "I guess we'll have to go back and look for her."

His voice was exasperated. They don't even care, thought Patricia. She wished she could tell Gordon and Rodney exactly what she thought of them.

"We have to get home," Paul apologized. "My mother's a light sleeper and she might get up and find out we're gone. There's no point in all of us staying, anyhow."

He and his sisters slipped away into the darkness. "Let us know what happens," whispered Barbara as they left. At least she sounded concerned.

Gordon, Rodney Tom and Patricia trudged back towards the camp. Rodney looked apprehensive. "It's dangerous to go too close to it. Maybe she's hiding in the bushes and she'll come out when she sees us."

"Or maybe she got caught," said Tom, voicing Patricia's thoughts.

Gordon stopped. "Someone's coming!"

They jumped into the bushes just in time. A grim-faced man, a raincoat flung over his pyjamas, was marching down the road. He clutched a flashlight in one hand and Ruth's arm in the other.

"You don't have to hold onto me," she told him coldly. "I'm not going to run away."

"You might. I won't risk letting you go until we get to your parents' place. I don't imagine they'll be too pleased, seeing what their daughter's been up to in the middle of the night."

After they passed the boys were silent for a few minutes. "Well, Turner, you're the lucky one," sighed Gordon finally. "You can still sneak in and no one will be any wiser." He stood up and brushed leaves off his pants. "Come on, Rodney—let's go home and face the fireworks."

RUTH'S MOTHER was always scolding her for one thing or another. But now her habitual irritation with her daughter boiled over. Patricia remembered Aunt Ginnie's brief outburst after the horse incident. That had been directed, clean anger. This was different; as if Ruth's misbehaviour had sparked a flame that fed on itself until it raged out of control.

She began berating her daughter at breakfast. Gordon looked worried. "Calm down, Ma," he entreated. "You're working yourself up into one of your states." But she angrily banished him and Rodney and Ginnie to the beach. Then she continued to rage.

"That a daughter of mine would do such a thing," was her constant refrain.

Nan's brittle voice drilled away at Ruth until Patricia wanted to scream. "I can't believe a daughter of mine would be so unladylike!" she repeated. "I don't know what to do with you, Ruth. You're twelve years old and here you are gallivanting off at night and behaving like a hoodlum!"

"The others did it, too," muttered Ruth.

Her mother had quickly found out who the others were.

"It's a disgrace that the Thorpe girls were there. They're exactly the kind of wild teenager you're turning into. As for Gordon and Rodney it's natural for boys to get up to mischief, but you had no business tagging along. I was mortified when that man appeared last night! The next thing we know, you'll be showing up with a policeman in tow. I won't have it, do you understand? I won't have my daughter behaving like this!"

Then she moved from last night to Ruth's whole character, bringing up incidents in her life from age two to the present. Nothing she described was really bad.

"Just because you're attractive, you've always thought you could get away with everything! Looks won't get you everything, you'll see. Sometimes I'd like to slap that pretty face of yours!"

Ruth looked as frightened as Patricia felt. Nan in the past was much, much worse than in the present. The furious woman paced wildly up and down the living room. It was as if she had come apart and didn't even know herself what she would say next.

At last, however, she took a deep breath as if trying to control herself. She stopped yelling and sent her daughter to her room. Ruth was to be confined to the cottage for the rest of the week.

That night Ruth cried for hours: dry, choked sobs that shook the bed. Patricia lay beside her helplessly, tears streaming down her own face.

When Andrew Reid arrived, his wife asked him to speak to his sons. He was mild with them. "Up to high jinks, eh? Just like your Uncle Wilfred. But you shouldn't have been there—you'd better write the camp a letter of apology."

Then he took his daughter aside. "I'm very disappointed that *you* were involved, Ruth. You've got to start mending your ways. You're making your mother very unhappy, and you know how agitated she can get. No one else in the family upsets her as much as you do—it's got to stop, do you hear?"

"But, Father, I don't *do* anything!" cried Ruth. "Not any more than the boys."

"But they're boys—you're not. You should know better. Now I won't put up with any more of it. The matter is closed."

He lit his pipe and dismissed her.

13

The atmosphere in the Reids' cottage was now so oppressive that the next time the watch ran down Patricia almost decided to stay in her own time. But the present, with Nan still there and her cousins' exuberance making her own troubles seem worse, was just as bad.

And she couldn't abandon Ruth now. Ruth had no one—even Ginnie ignored her much of the time. She was alone, whereas Patricia—she squirmed guiltily at the realization—had Aunt Ginnie and Uncle Doug and, recently even Kelly all wanting to befriend her. But I don't need them, she thought stubbornly as much as Ruth needs *me.*

How could she comfort Ruth, though, when Ruth didn't know she was there? Maybe she could leave her a note. But what could it say? "Dear Ruth, I'm your daughter Patricia ..." No, a note would only confuse or frighten Ruth. If only it were possible to act, to somehow express her sympathy towards the miserable girl. She felt useless. It was a familiar feeling, but she was weary of it.

No wonder ghosts were sad; they were removed from living. It occurred to Patricia that not only was she a ghost in the past, she was like one in the present as well. There was no longer anywhere to escape to.

"Your punishment is over, Ruth," said her mother after a week. Her frightening anger had subsided and she was back to her usual impassive self.

She began to discuss the costume party that was taking place on the coming weekend. Patricia cheered up a little; maybe the past would become interesting again.

"We have to think of something to wear and I have an easy idea," said Nan. "Why don't we dress up as each other? I'll be Father and he can be me. Gordon and Ginnie can trade clothes … and so can Ruth and Rodney."

Ginnie exploded into laughter. "Gordie *me*? Will he wear one of my dresses? How will he get it on?"

At first the boys flatly refused to dress up as girls, but their mother finally persuaded them. Ruth shrugged an agreement to wearing Rodney's clothes. She had become sullen and silent since the awful scolding.

"It's settled, then. I'll call your father from the store phone and ask him to bring some of our city clothes out."

On Saturday evening Patricia watched the family get ready for the party. Ginnie became so choked with hilarity they had to slap her on the back. Even Andrew Reid snorted at himself in the mirror. This must be one of the "happy times" Aunt Ginnie recalled. She didn't know that one person in the family hadn't been happy. An unsmiling Ruth quickly donned Rodney's knitted vest, wide tie and grey flannels, then retreated to her puzzle until the others were dressed.

"We must have a picture," said Nan. "Where's your Brownie, Gordon?"

Gordon produced a box-like camera. They asked the next-door neighbour, a younger Mrs. Donaldson, to come over and snap them on the front steps. Patricia watched as intently as if she were taking the picture herself. With a shiver, she recalled the evening Aunt Ginnie had shown her the photograph. Then the black-and-white picture had seemed long ago. Now the family group was like a commercial: in "full, living colour."

"I think you'll win first prize!" said Mrs. Donaldson. "You're quite a sight."

They were. Rodney's fairness suited the pink dress of Ruth's he was wearing, even though his gangly wrists hung far below the sleeves. They'd concocted a little girl's outfit for Gordon out of one of Ginnie's pinafores, tied loosely around his chest and layered with several aprons. Wool pigtails dangled over his ears and he cradled her doll. Ginnie giggled in Gordon's rolled up pants and brandished his badminton racquet proudly. Ruth stood sullenly between her brothers, submerged in Rodney's baggy clothes.

"Perhaps I'll start wearing dresses, eh, Ginnie?" joked her father. "They're really quite comfortable."

"Not as comfortable as trousers," declared his wife. "Just a minute, Sally," she said to Mrs. Donaldson. "I've forgotten something."

She hurried into the cottage and returned smiling. "There! What do you think? It's a man's watch, after all."

Across her husband's vest hung a gold chain, one end pinned to the dark material. She drew out the watch to show them, then replaced it carefully in her vest pocket.

"The perfect touch," agreed Mrs. Donaldson. "Now, are you all ready? Smile, Ruth!"

She didn't, but the picture was taken anyway.

THE RECREATION HALL was new to Patricia; it was connected to the store and also built out of logs. Tonight it was crammed with noisy families, all in costume. The Thorpe children, draped in pink beach towels, came as The Three Little Pigs. Barbara and Winnie teased Ruth's brothers about their girls' clothes. The boys' cheeks burned, but Patricia could tell they enjoyed the attention.

At one end of the hall was a long table piled with cookies, pies and lemonade. In the corner two older men began a lively tune on an accordian and fiddle.

"If only we had electricity at the lake," complained Gordon. "Father could have brought some of my jazz albums from the city."

People began dancing. Andrew Reid polkaed with Ginnie in his arms, her legs wrapped around his waist. Nan claimed Rodney and Gordon asked Barbara.

Patricia followed Ruth over to the refreshments. Ruth looked shy, the way she herself always felt at a party. This gathering, however, was the most relaxed one she had ever been to. Excited greetings and laughter competed with the music. Small children pushed past the adults and clustered around the food. Two dogs wearing hats hung around them hopefully.

A woman grinned at Ruth, baring false teeth cut out of an orange peel. "What a clever idea your costumes are, Ruth. It's hard to come up with something when you're not in the city."

"My mother thought of it," mumbled Ruth.

"Hey, Ruth!" Tom appeared at her side. "Who are you disguised as?"

"Rodney," grimaced Ruth. "The person I'd least like to be. We all had to come as one another. You look funny," she added hesitantly.

Tom was dressed as a baby. He hoisted up a drooping diaper made out of a sheet. "Our family's the Dionne Quintuplets. We have lots of bottles around because of my little sister. Here, have a sip." He thrust a baby bottle towards her.

Ruth made a face, but Tom insisted. "Ugh!" she shuddered. "That's not milk!"

"It is, but I added some brandy."

The accordian player announced that the judging had begun. One at a time, individuals and groups presented themselves at the front of the room. "And here are the Reids ... dressed as the Reids!" someone cried as the family posed. They won third prize, outshone by a bandaged mummy and five children, swamped in their fathers' uniforms, who carried a sign saying What We Fought For—The Future Generation.

Then square dancing began. Patricia enjoyed watching the intricate patterns each group formed. She clapped her hands in time. "Now do-si-do and promenade ..." The caller's orders were so intriguing, she almost didn't notice Tom whispering to Ruth beside her.

"Listen, Ruth. This party's a bore. Some of us are sneaking out and going to the beach—want to come?"

Ruth looked for her parents, part of a set at the other end of the hall. Ginnie was sprawled on a mattress amidst some other small children, stuffing cookies into her mouth.

"I suppose so," said Ruth nervously. "I'd have to get back before the party's over, though—my parents are really strict."

"Don't worry, we won't stay long," Tom assured her. Patricia followed them out a side door. Three other couples were waiting in the darkness. One pair was Rodney and Winnie. The others were strangers, all in their mid-teens.

They trooped after the beam of Tom's flashlight down the path to the Main Beach. Two of the boys gathered branches and made a fire and soon everyone was huddled around it.

Tom passed around his baby bottle and someone else produced beer. "Don't you dare drink anything," Rodney warned his sister. "You shouldn't have come. She's only twelve, you know," he told Tom.

"I don't like beer," retorted Ruth. "But you shouldn't be drinking either. So shut up, or I'll tell on you."

Surprisingly, Rodney did.

"Where's Gordon?" Ruth asked him after a while.

"He and Barbara left to go to a dance across the lake. Father lent him the car. Gordon arranged it yesterday and didn't even tell me," he added bitterly.

The group sat self-consciously around the fire, hardly speaking. One of the boys slung his arm around the girl beside him. Everyone pretended not to notice. They coughed over a shared cigarette and made a few remarks about the childishness of the costume party but the voices sounded wistful. Patricia was surprised at their awkwardness; she had always thought that everyone but herself was confident in situations like this.

A loon laughed on the lake. "It's getting cold," said Winnie, wrapping her towel around her. "Let's go back."

Everyone looked relieved. "At least the grub's great," said one of the boys on the way up the steps. "Have you tried my aunt's sausage rolls?"

Ahead of them the hall's windows flickered with candlelight. Voices boomed out into the night: "Pack up your troubles in your old kit bag / And smile, smile, smile ..." When she got back into the noisy warmth, Patricia sang along.

"No one will even guess we left," said Tom with satisfaction. He wolfed down some pie.

But Ruth looked worried. "I can't see my parents anywhere. Can you?"

Patricia's eyes searched with her. There was no sign of any of the Reids.

"Rodney!" Ruth cornered her brother. "Where are Mother and Father?"

Rodney became anxious as well. He approached a woman dressed as a gypsy. "Excuse me, Mrs. Duffy, have you seen our parents?"

"Oh, there you are, you two!" The woman pretended to be stern. "Your mother and father just left. Ginnie was sick to her stomach—too much cake, I expect. They were looking for you. Your father's coming back after he walks Pat and Ginnie home. You'd better get going," she admonished.

"Oh, no," groaned Rodney. Then he looked resigned. "Listen, Ruth. If I'm going to get into trouble anyway, I may as well stay. There's a party at Winnie's cousins' afterwards. It's you they'll be worried about. Go back and tell them I promise to be home by midnight."

Ruth bristled. "You always do this!" she hissed. "I get blamed for everything and you get away with murder. It's not fair! Besides, I don't want to walk back alone in the dark. You have to come too, Rodney."

Winnie and Tom had joined them and Winnie took Rodney's arm, frowning at Ruth as if she were a tiresome little girl.

"I'll take you home, Ruth," offered Tom. "I don't mind."

"Gee, thanks, Turner." Rodney bolted with Winnie before his friend could change his mind.

Patricia hurried to keep up with Ruth as she stomped ahead of Tom on the road. "I despise Rodney!" she growled. "He treats me like a child. They all do. It's just like the raid."

"What happened about that?" asked Tom. "Were your parents angry?"

"They were furious, especially my mother. But not at Gordon and Rodney—they didn't get into trouble at all. It'll be the same thing tonight. She'll yell at me for days, but nothing will happen to Rodney."

"It's just because you're a girl. My little sisters get the same treatment. But girls need to be taken care of, you know. I'm glad I'm not one," he added cheerfully.

Ruth whirled around and faced him. "I don't need taking care of! You can just leave, Tom Turner! I can walk home by myself!"

"You *are* a wildcat, aren't you?" said Tom calmly. "Relax. It's pretty dark and I have the flashlight. You may as well put up with me."

Ruth ignored him as they continued walking. Tom whistled and played with his flashlight, beaming it to the tops of trees and into ditches. "Got to be careful of skunks," he commented. "There's lots, around at this time of year."

Ruth wouldn't answer. Their footsteps were muffled in the soft dust of the road. Soon they could hear voices ahead: two adults and a piping child singing "The Teddybears' Picnic."

"It's my parents," muttered Ruth. "Slow down. I don't feel like facing them yet."

Tom pointed his flashlight to the ground. Then he paused. "Hey ... what's that?" Something on the side of the road glittered as it caught the light.

He stooped and picked it up. "It's a watch! Looks pretty valuable."

Ruth snatched it from him. "It's my mother's. She was wearing it tonight … it must have come unpinned."

"Why was your mother wearing a man's watch?"

"Well, she was dressed as a man, wasn't she? But it's her watch. Her fiancé gave it to her. He died, and then she married my father."

"She must really care for it, then."

"She likes this stupid watch better than anything," said Ruth bitterly. "Better than …" Her voice petered out and she fingered the chain thoughtfully.

"She'll be glad you found it, then," said Tom. "That's a point in your favour."

"Yes, she'd hate to lose this watch," said Ruth slowly. "She'd be really miserable." Patricia shuddered at the strangeness in her voice.

"Here we are." Tom stopped at the end of the Reids' driveway. "You won't want your parents to see me, so I'll leave you here." He cleared his throat. "I'm sorry you're mad at me … I like you. If I was going to be here for the rest of the summer we could do things together, but we've just sold our cottage. Next month we're moving to Ontario so I guess I won't be seeing you anymore, Ruth."

He sounded awkward, especially since Ruth was paying no attention to him. Patricia felt sorry for him. Tom was conceited and he had irritating ideas about girls, but he seemed to genuinely care for Ruth. If she were Ruth she would be nicer to him.

But Ruth just kept staring at the watch. "Well, good-bye, then," Tom continued. "I hope you don't get into trouble."

"I will," Ruth said gloomily, looking up at last. "Thanks for walking me home," she added absent-mindedly.

Tom suddenly grabbed Ruth's shoulders and kissed her on the mouth. Then he ran fast down the road.

Patricia waited curiously for Ruth's reaction, but all Ruth did was touch her mouth with the back of her hand, a surprised expression on her face. Then she shrugged and turned up the driveway.

Now for another tongue-lashing, sighed Patricia. She heard excited voices coming from the cottage. Probably Nan had already noticed the missing watch. But maybe she'd be so relieved when Ruth gave it back, she wouldn't be angry with her daughter for leaving the party.

Ruth, however, didn't go up to the cottage. She opened the door of La Petite and entered the small, dark space. Just as Patricia followed her in, Andrew Reid's voice called, "Get the child to bed. I'll look in the driveway before I go back for Ruth."

Ruth stood inside the cabin, gazing at the watch in her palm. Then she took short rapid steps in all directions, peering into corners as if she were looking for something.

All at once Patricia guessed what she was about to do. She remembered Nan's sad voice telling them how she had lost the watch "through my own carelessness."

If she had lost it, then Ruth had never given it back.

Ruth knelt down on the floor and ran her hands over it. She hesitated a second, then searched her pockets and drew out Rodney's large white handkerchief. Wrapping the watch and chain in it, she lifted up a floorboard and laid the bundle carefully into the cavity underneath. Then she dropped the board on top. She raised her head and looked directly at Patricia, her vivid face flaming with triumph and guilt.

On the way back to the cottage Patricia waited while Ruth detoured to the outhouse. She reappeared just as her father came striding down the driveway with a large flashlight.

He directed it upon his daughter. "Ruth! Where have you been? You're in a lot of trouble, young lady! Your mother's beside herself. She's lost—"

Patricia didn't hear any more. In the next instant she was sitting in the attic in the mid-morning sunlight.

14

"Not *now*!" Patricia cried aloud. The watch always ran down just before lunch, never at night. She must have only wound it halfway last time.

She yanked the chain over her head and clutched the warm gold disk in her sweaty hands. Her fingers slipped on the knob as they twisted, twisted, twisted … She had to get back to Ruth at once and see what happened to her.

She turned her fingers even more frantically and the winding mechanism clicked faster and faster. Then her thumb snapped past her forefinger as the knob lost its friction and revolved too easily. It felt loose and empty and turned backwards as well as forwards.

She'd broken it. The knob had lost its connection with whatever it turned inside. In vain, Patricia shook and tapped the metal case, opened it up, jiggled it and held it to her ear with a desperate hope. But the watch was dead.

She dashed down the attic stairs to the kitchen. There was the modern stove and fridge and the door to the bathroom. The sun blazed through the windows and bounced off the shiny electric kettle.

Patricia ran out to check La Petite, but it was the same. Nan's things were neatly placed on the dresser and chair. A mosquito whined in the still air. The floor, under which she had just witnessed Ruth hiding the watch, was sealed with the shiny new tiles Uncle Doug had laid.

Take me back! Patricia implored, shaking the watch again. Something rattled inside; she knew it was truly broken.

She rushed out of the cabin and down to the beach, crawled under the canoe, stretched out on the cold pebbles and cried.

She would never see Ruth again. She would never know what had happened to her that night or for the rest of that summer. And she would never again be as safe, concealed and free as she had been. The adventure was over, and the person she had felt closest to in her life, troubled, rebellious, spirited Ruth, was gone.

After a while Patricia stopped crying and reflected on Ruth's act of revenge. She had been so sure that Ruth was going to return the watch to win her mother's approval. Even though Patricia felt just as angry with Nan, Ruth's deliberate cruelty shocked her. She wondered why she hadn't simply hidden the watch for a few days, then "found" it. Ruth's mother would have been so grateful that she'd have forgiven her daughter's transgressions and the stormy relationship might have improved. Patricia wondered if Ruth had ever felt guilty, in all the years following her decision. She felt guilty herself, knowing.

The long day wore on and the family talked about Nan leaving tomorrow. Patricia kept the watch concealed under her clothes and began to consider if she should give it back to her grandmother. It was no use to her anymore. Maybe doing so might somehow help make things better between Nan, her mother and her.

But Ruth had chosen not to. Should she respect that choice? Yet it *was* Nan's watch.... That night she tossed hotly under the heavy quilt as she wrestled with the problem.

"You're keeping me awake," Kelly complained sleepily.

"Sorry." Forcing herself to be still, Patricia lay on her back, the watch sliding sideways under her nightgown. Her tears returned as she became overwhelmed by all it stood for: the lost past it contained and the impossible decision it seemed to be asking her to make.

"Why are you crying, Patricia?" Kelly sat up and stared at her cousin. Patricia didn't even try to stop. Her body quaked and she sniffed noisily.

"Should I get Mum?"

Patricia shook her head.

"I'll get you a kleenex, then." Kelly padded out of the room and returned with a handful of toilet paper. "Sorry—no more kleenex. It's your parents, isn't it? Don't worry, Patricia, everything will work out."

Kelly thumped her cousin on the back as heartily as if she were Peggy. Patricia blew her nose and tucked the wad of toilet paper under her pillow. "Th-thanks," she murmured, swallowing the rest of her sobs. "I'm all right now." Kelly looked relieved and settled back to sleep.

When she thought it was safe, Patricia let herself cry again, but now her tears were not as urgent. They drained out like the last bit of water in a tub. Part of her noted dully that, for the first time, Kelly hadn't called her Potty.

BY THE TIME Nan left, Patricia knew she couldn't return the watch. Not yet, anyway. She tried to control her guilt by reminding herself that it wasn't *her* fault the watch was lost; it was Ruth's. The decision could wait. At the end of the summer, maybe, she would give it to Aunt Ginnie to return to her mother. Right now she longed too much for the past to let the watch go; it was all she had left. Besides, she couldn't help hoping that somehow it would begin to tick again.

As Nan hugged her granddaughter's stiff body, all of Patricia's bitter feelings arose again. Now she was glad she was keeping the watch from her; she tasted some of Ruth's revenge.

"Dear Patricia," Nan crooned. "I'm sorry we didn't have time to become friends, but we will. Next summer I'm going to insist you come and visit me, especially now that your mother will be alone. It will help her out."

"I have to stay in Toronto next summer," Patricia lied. "There's a special course I have to take."

Uncle Doug started the engine and everyone waved. "Goodbye, Nan!" called Trevor, sprinting beside the car.

It was a relief to have her gone. Even Aunt Ginnie seemed to feel it. "I love seeing your grandmother," she confided to Kelly and Patricia as they helped her strip the bed in La Petite, "but I don't think she enjoys the lake anymore. She doesn't like being as informal as we are in the summer."

"That's for sure—a fork for ice cream!" said Kelly scornfully. Every night Nan had insisted that Kelly set the table with a spoon and fork for each person's dessert.

"Now, Kelly," admonished her mother, "she can't help that. When people are old they often become set in their ways. She's a kind person and she loves you all dearly."

"Well, Patricia and I are glad she's gone, aren't we? Come on, let's go find the others." Kelly pulled Patricia out of La Petite before Aunt Ginnie could scold her.

FOR THE NEXT two weeks Patricia was numb with grief. Her longing for Ruth and the past was such a sharp pain that she moved around slowly so as not to aggravate it. Once she thought of taking the watch somewhere to be fixed, but there were no watchmakers or jewellers listed in the thin town phonebook. She gave up hope that it would work again and put it away in the attic.

In a forlorn daze, Patricia tagged after her cousins as they finished their fort and began building a raft. It wasn't until the beginning of August, as she lay on her stomach on Uncle Rod's pier and listened to the others hammering behind her, that she realized she was now accepted.

No one dangled small animals in her face. No one called her Potty. When Maggie had, Kelly said fiercely, "Don't use that dumb name anymore. She doesn't like it." Maggie compromised on "Patty" instead.

They felt sorry for her. Patricia was sure that Kelly had told Christie and Bruce about her parents and that was the reason why they, too, were being friendly and patient. She had to admit that she had not returned their friendliness; she just watched, as usual. No one minded. They treated her like glass, like an invalid who might break.

There's nothing *wrong* with me, thought Patricia resentfully. They don't need to be so careful. She sat up and brushed flying bugs away from her face. Trevor panted as he moved along the boards, hammering each one to a horizontal plank underneath. His plump sunburnt back quivered with each blow.

Patricia went over to him. "Do you want me to do that for a while?"

"Sure! Gee, it's hot!" Trevor handed her the hammer and plunged into the lake.

Patricia pounded carefully, copying Kelly and Christie's rhythmic strokes at the other end. It was a relief to do something and satisfying to watch the wooden platform grow as they added boards.

"There!" Kelly sat back and wiped her dripping face. "That's great, Patricia. Now we just need to find some inner tubes to hold it up in the water." She grinned at her cousin and Patricia smiled back tentatively.

15

*T*hen began the only restful part of Patricia's summer. The past and the future were both too disturbing to contemplate: she couldn't dwell on Ruth without being heartbroken and she dared not think of what awaited her in Toronto. It was easiest simply to exist in the present.

She and Kelly were now friends. Patricia admired her cousin's strong principles on everything from the peace movement to how to split a popsicle without breaking it. Kelly had even written a letter to the prime minister stating her concerns about nuclear war.

"My mother did a special series on disarmament," Patricia told her.

"I saw it! I didn't tell you … before."

Before we were friends, Patricia added to herself.

"I'm sorry we were so mean to you when you came," Kelly told her sheepishly. "You were so snotty, we thought you didn't like us."

"But I thought you didn't like *me*!"

"Well, I was upset because of not getting a sailboat. I guess we didn't give you a chance." Kelly grinned at her. "But now we know each other. And we're cousins, so we always will."

The two of them began talking long into the night. Kelly told Patricia what interesting lives her friends with divorced parents had. "Sometimes I think it's a drag, having such an ordinary family." She didn't sound at all convincing, but Patricia appreciated her efforts to cheer her up.

They chatted so late that Aunt Ginnie threatened to separate them, but she looked indulgent as she said it. Her aunts and uncles beamed on Patricia now. "The lake has done her good," she heard Aunt Karen say. "She's a changed child."

Sometimes Patricia sneaked up to the attic and tried the watch again. But it was definitely broken. Once she visited the badminton court, straining her ears as if she could hear Ruth's voice cry again: "It's not fair!" The overgrown, neglected space was silent.

Each August day dawned with a clean, blue sky. By noon it was hot, but the evenings were crisp, with none of the stifling humidity Patricia was used to in Toronto. Swimming lessons were over and nothing in the day was organized but meals. The cousins spent every possible moment outside, either in the fort or on the beach. Patricia's hair grew into her eyes, her skin turned brown and the soles of her feet became as hard as Kelly's. She wasn't afraid of weeds or bloodsuckers anymore, she could paddle a canoe and she caught another perch. I'm getting as good as they are, she thought.

Her cousins continued to protect her, however. "You won't like this, Patricia," Bruce warned when he showed the others his worm farm. "Patricia doesn't have to do it,"

ordered Kelly, when they dared one another to dive off
the high board on the Main Beach raft. Patricia was grateful for their concern; she still didn't have the nerve to do
everything they did. But she wished she could win their
respect as well as their sympathy.

After lunch one day Aunt Karen rushed through the
back door of the Grants' cottage. "Bruce cut his foot with
the axe! It's bleeding a lot. Ginnie, can you drive us to the
hospital in Stony Plain? If only Rod was here!"

They all ran out to the driveway. Bruce was lying on
the back seat of the car. Christie was beside him, holding
a blood-soaked towel to his foot. He looked up weakly
and tried to smile. "Gee, my blood's sure red."

"Oh, B-Bruce ..." wailed his sister.

"Christie, let your mother do that," said Aunt Ginnie.
Aunt Karen gathered her son in her arms.

Aunt Ginnie handed the baby to Kelly. "Maggie, run
and get my purse. Now listen carefully, you older ones.
We'll probably be gone until dinner-time. Rosemary's
formula is in the cupboard by the sink. You shouldn't have
any problems, but go to Mrs. Donaldson if you do.
There's lots of food for snacks ... I'm sure you'll manage."

Maggie returned with the purse. "You do exactly what
Kelly says," her mother told her. She scrambled into the
driver's seat and backed the car down the driveway, Peggy
following it yelping and jumping.

Rosemary's eyes widened with astonishment at the
sight of her retreating mother. Then she opened her
mouth and took a deep breath.

"Oh-oh," said Kelly, jiggling her desperately. The cry seemed to take forever to emerge. When it did, it pierced Patricia's ears. The baby's face turned crimson as her screams became regular.

"Let's take her inside." The others followed Kelly into the living room and slouched around the baby as she continued to thrash and wail.

"*Do* something!" Trevor entreated his sister, his lingers plugging his ears. "You're in charge."

Kelly bounced the baby higher. "I don't *know* what to do! She never carries on like this."

Christie cried too, softly in a corner, while Maggie brought all of Rosemary's toys to her and waved them in her face.

Patricia watched until she couldn't bear it. She took a steadying breath and stood up. "Stop that, Maggie. You're just making her worse. Give her to me, Kelly."

Kelly looked surprised, but handed the baby over with relief.

"Go and heat up some formula," ordered Patricia, folding her arms around Rosemary and trying to still the small, shaking body.

Kelly looked embarrassed. "How?"

Patricia led them into the kitchen and directed her. Kelly opened the tin of formula and heated it slowly in a pot. Trevor helped funnel it into a bottle. But Rosemary would have no part of it. She spat out the nipple and screamed even louder.

"She's not hungry," said Patricia. "Your Mum just weaned her anyhow—she's not used to the bottle."

"Get Mrs. Donaldson!" urged Trevor.

"She isn't there," said Maggie. "I just went over."

The others watched as Patricia tried everything. She checked Rosemary's diaper, took her outside, walked her up and down and sang to her. Nothing worked.

"Please, please stop," she whispered helplessly into the baby's neck, close to tears herself. She tried to think clearly. What made Rosemary happy?

"I know! Run the bath, quick! Not too full and not very hot." She pulled off the baby's clothes as Kelly turned on the taps. She tested the water. Then, holding the baby carefully under her neck and ankles as Aunt Ginnie did, she lowered her into it.

It was a miracle. As soon as she felt the warm water Rosemary's cries diminished into hiccups. Then there was a wonderful silence. She moved her arms and legs around and started to smile.

"You're a genius, Patricia!" marvelled Kelly. "How did you think of it?" She splashed her sister's fat stomach and Rosemary laughed.

"Well, I know she loves baths. I guess she just needed to be distracted."

They kept her in the tub as long as possible, then dressed her apprehensively, terrified she'd begin again. But Rosemary was exhausted. As Patricia rocked her she closed her eyes.

Patricia laid her carefully in her crib and shut the door. "Whew!" She collapsed in the rocking chair. Her cousins were all gazing at her with respect and expectancy. All but Christie, who continued to sob.

"Oh, poor, poor Bruce. What if he loses his foot?"

Patricia made herself speak with confidence. "Listen, Christie—all of you. I have an idea. Let's make a special dinner for them. There's a chicken in the fridge, I saw it.'

"But we don't know how to cook a chicken," said Kelly.

"I can. I do it all the time at home. And we'll have boiled potatoes and green beans and a salad and chocolate pudding. You can all help."

Christie stopped sniffing as she and Trevor peeled potatoes. Patricia made a bread stuffing and got Kelly to trim the beans and Maggie to pick flowers for the table. She was amazed that they let her be the leader so easily.

After she'd put the stuffed chicken into the oven, Rosemary woke up. Patricia fed her while she told Kelly how to make the pudding. "… And now just stir until it thickens," she finished.

"How do you *know* all this?" asked her cousin. "Why didn't you tell us you could cook?"

"My … father taught me. I did try to tell you once." That time in the canoe seemed ages ago.

"He's a great teacher. You're as good as Mum!"

Patricia glowed. She lifted Rosemary to her shoulder and burped her, feeling as peaceful as the baby.

A FEW HOURS LATER the two aunts walked into the kitchen supporting Bruce between them. His foot was bandaged neatly and his T-shirt was smeared with ice cream.

Christie rushed at Aunt Karen. "Everything's fine," she laughed.

"Bruce had to have a few stitches, but we think he'll live," said Aunt Ginnie, taking the baby in her arms. "What's that fantastic smell? Karen, look what they've done!"

"Come and sit down, please," said Maggie gravely. She led them to their places, each one marked with a place card she'd decorated. Bruce had the seat of honour, his chair covered in ribbons and flowers.

Kelly, Christie and Trevor carried in the vegetables that had been kept warm in the oven. Patricia set the chicken in front of her aunt, its skin crisp and glistening.

"You'll have to carve it," she said shyly. "I don't know how." She placed a pitcher of gravy beside it.

"You wonderful children!" cried Aunt Karen. "How did you manage to do all this?"

"*Patricia* did it," they chorused. "And she got the Piglet to stop crying," added Kelly. "*She's* wonderful."

Patricia gazed at the circle of faces around the table as they drank her a toast with ginger ale.

This is my family, she thought. This is a place where I belong.

THAT WEEKEND was Uncle Doug's birthday and both families had a barbecue on the beach to celebrate. The meal, planned by Aunt Ginnie and Patricia, was a huge success.

"Thank you all for a wonderful feast," said Uncle Doug. He strummed softly on his guitar while the children lay on their backs, patting their full stomachs. They were watching for falling stars.

"This is the best time of year for them," said Bruce. "The Perseid meteor shower, is that right, Dad?"

His father looked embarrassed. "I'm not sure, son. Your Uncle Gordon should be here—he's the one who knows about stars. We used to have a telescope, but he took it to Victoria with him."

"There's Scorpius," pointed out Patricia. "See its tail?"

Uncle Rod glanced at her with surprise. "You're a mysterious one. Where did you learn that?"

Patricia shrugged and dared to return his curious look.

Maggie lay with her head in her mother's lap, chanting:

Star light, star bright
First star I see tonight
Wish I may wish I might
Have the wish I wish tonight.
I wish that ...

She squeezed her eyes shut.

Patricia decided to wish too. It took her a few minutes to decide on one. She could wish that her parents wouldn't separate; but she knew that they would, and even that they should. What she wanted the most would never come true, but it wouldn't hurt to try.

I wish I could see Ruth again, she thought.

"There's a moving one!" cried Bruce. Patricia opened her eyes and saw a speck of light slide across the darkness. Soon the night sky was alive with darting silver streaks.

"Star light, star bright, twelfth star I see tonight!" crowed Maggie. Everyone groaned.

"Can't you stop now, Maggie?" asked Uncle Doug. "It's only the first star that counts."

"How do you know?" demanded Maggie. Her father had to admit he didn't.

"She's probably wishing for money," said Trevor. Maggie glared at him, so they knew he was right.

Patricia stuck another marshmallow on her stick. Kelly and Christie were burning theirs, having a contest to see how many gooey layers they could get under each black skin. But Patricia liked trying to toast hers an even brown, the way she'd once watched Ruth do it.

"Thirtieth star I see tonight …" Maggie's voice murmured to a stop and her eyes stayed closed.

"What are all you young ones going to be when you grow up?" Uncle Rod asked them.

"A lawyer like Grandfather Reid," Kelly said promptly.

"A horse trainer," said Christie just as fast.

Bruce examined his foot and said maybe he'd be a doctor. Trevor yawned placidly. "Who knows?"

"Maggie will be rich, of course," Uncle Rod chuckled. "What about our little Easterner?"

Patricia tried not to mumble. "Maybe I could run a restaurant."

"Yum!" said Kelly "You'd be good at it?"

"Or maybe …" Patricia stopped, flushing.

"Go on, dear," encouraged Aunt Ginnie.

"Maybe I'll be a mother," she said softly. She thought of being in on a baby like Rosemary right from the beginning.

Kelly hooted. "But you can be *more* than just a mother, silly. You can have a career, too. Look at your mum. She's really successful and she had you."

"I guess so …" Patricia remembered one day when she and her mother had both been home with the flu. How they'd read aloud to each other and watched TV in the big bed … how relaxing it had been to have a whole day loosened from its usual tight schedule.

"We come on the sloop *John B.*," crooned Uncle Doug. The family joined in. Patricia sang the chorus quietly as she leaned against Aunt Ginnie.

Let me go home
Let me go home
I feel so broke up
I want to go home.

But I don't want to go home, she thought. There were only two weeks left to the summer. She wanted to freeze it, to stay at the lake forever—on this beach where her mother, too, had once sat.

Trevor and Christie had fallen asleep now. Their fathers picked them up and everyone climbed the steps to the cottage.

"Patricia, dear, will you wait up a minute?" Aunt Ginnie asked her. She carried Maggie to her bed, then thanked Mrs. Donaldson, who had come over with her knitting to listen for Rosemary.

Patricia sat dreamily on the verandah, listening to the loon's lonely call. Everyone else went to bed, then Aunt Ginnie joined her.

"I had an exciting message this afternoon and I wanted to tell you first." Her aunt's eyes sparkled. "Can you guess?"

Patricia shook her head, puzzled.

"It's your mother—she's coming for a visit! She says she has something important to discuss with you. She's flying to Edmonton on Sunday and you and Uncle Doug can go in and pick her up. What a treat it will be to have her here after all these years!"

Aunt Ginnie babbled on while Patricia sat in a stunned silence, unable to say a word.

16

"*I*s your mother a movie star?" asked Maggie. Trevor caught a plate she was about to drop. "Dummie! She's on TV, not the movies. We keep telling you that, Maggie. But she's famous, isn't she, Patricia?"

They were doing the lunch dishes and listening for the car containing Uncle Doug and Patricia's mother to arrive. Patricia had backed out of going to the airport.

"I understand," Aunt Ginnie reassured her. "Airports are so impersonal … you'd rather meet her here." She seemed to think Patricia was as easygoing with her mother as Kelly was with her.

Guiltily, Patricia tried to suppress the resentment she felt about her mother's visit. It was spoiling everything. Her coming meant the end of the short period when she had almost been content. It also meant the end of the summer.

She wondered how her mother had managed to find time off from her busy schedule. What was she going to discuss? Her parents had probably reached some decisions now about some of the unpleasant things, like visiting rights, that Kelly's friends had to cope with. It would be so embarrassing, talking about it.

They heard Peggy's joyful bark, the one that meant, "My car's here!"

"Leave the dishes," smiled Aunt Ginnie, hurrying through the kitchen with Rosemary. "They've arrived!"

Patricia lagged behind. She watched a tall, elegant figure, impeccably dressed in a beige linen suit, step out of the car and kiss Aunt Ginnie on the cheek.

"Here are your nieces and your nephew!" cried Aunt Ginnie. Her voice was unnaturally high and nervous. "And here's Patricia!"

They all stepped aside to let Patricia through. "Hi, Mum," she said in a low voice. She waited to be kissed.

"Hello, darling." Her mother leaned forward and pecked her daughter. Then she examined her for a moment, and Patricia had to steady herself with the shock. She was looking into the younger Ruth's grey eyes. These eyes, though, were skilfully made up and self-assured, filled with controlled impatience.

The other Ruth's vulnerable, restless personality, continually squashed by her family, had evoked Patricia's deepest sympathies. Nobody squashed this Ruth. Her manicured confidence cancelled out her younger self. In the instant of confronting her mother, the past crumbled away. It was as if Patricia had never known the younger Ruth; the grown-up one, with whom she had lived all her life, was so much more powerful.

Now she felt cheated and angry. And to make things worse, she heard with dismay that Aunt Ginnie was moving her into La Petite "so the two of you can have some privacy." She sat on the edge of one of the beds with Kelly and Maggie and watched her mother unpack. With a smirk of superiority, Patricia wondered if all she had brought were linen suits.

But her mother always knew how to dress. She changed into cotton walking shorts and a short-sleeved flowered blouse. Her clothes still looked much too well-pressed and clean for the lake. There was a big difference between her appearance and theirs.

"Look at you three!" she said crisply. "You're little savages. What on earth are you wearing, Patricia? Where are all the new shorts I bought for you? And you need a haircut badly."

Patricia glanced down at the pair of Kelly's cut-offs she was wearing. She flicked her bangs off her forehead sullenly Kelly was in a holey bathing suit and all Maggie had on were Trevor's shorts, back to front.

"It's all right, Aunt Ruth," said Kelly cheerfully. "We never bother about clothes in the summer."

"You won't be able to go on TV when you're here," Maggie told her earnestly, "because we haven't got one."

Patricia's mother laughed. "I guess I won't, Maggie. Well, I need a holiday."

"Do you make a lot of money?" the little girl asked her.

"Can you pick the people you interview?" Kelly wanted to know.

Their aunt chatted easily with them. Patricia wasn't surprised; her mother was always charming. The day she had come and spoken to Patricia's school, everyone had raved about her. Patricia knew they wondered why her daughter was so different.

She supposed her mother was charming to her, too, the way she always called her "darling." Nan had used the term too. Patricia realized that she had always hated that word. Whatever she was, she wasn't darling. Saying it all the time meant her mother couldn't see what she was really like underneath.

"Your mum's nice," whispered Kelly as they all walked up the driveway. "Kind of proper, but she's okay."

Patricia watched her mother closely as she peered around the cottage. She wondered how much she remembered, especially since the place had not altered much.

Kelly pointed out her bedroom.

"This was my room!" said Patricia's mother. "What a long time has passed.... I think I last slept in here when I was seventeen."

"What happened then?" asked Kelly.

"I left home to go East to university."

"But didn't you come back for the holidays?"

Patricia was surprised to see her mother flush. "It was too expensive, so I worked in Toronto every summer."

After the tour of the cottage, Uncle Doug and his children went for a ride in Mr. Donaldson's motorboat. Aunt Ginnie took her sister for a walk, Patricia pushing the baby in her carriage.

"I can paddle a canoe," she said casually, as they watched a red one on the water below them. "And I caught two fish."

Her mother looked surprised. "Really, darling? I didn't think you liked that sort of thing."

"Oh, we've turned Patricia into a real little tomboy," chuckled Aunt Ginnie. "Kelly's influence, I'm afraid, but it's been good for her."

Patricia stomped her hard, bare feet along the path haughtily. In two months she'd accomplished as much as Rosemary, who could now turn over both ways and almost sit up.

"I used to be able to paddle a canoe," mused Patricia's mother. "I'm sure I've forgotten now."

"Later you and Patricia can take out the *Loon,*" suggested Aunt Ginnie.

"The *Loon*?" Patricia's mother looked puzzled until her sister explained.

How could she forget? Patricia thought angrily. She used to love the canoe; now she was speaking about her summers here as if they had happened to another person.

They had set out for the Main Beach, but Patricia's mother wanted to go back for her hat. "The sun's so bad for your skin," she explained, "and I don't like the look of that peeling nose, Patricia. You need some sunscreen on it."

Aunt Ginnie looked guilty. "Oh dear, it *is* burnt. I have such a hard time keeping them all protected."

They changed direction. "You haven't lost any weight, darling," Patricia's mother remarked.

"She takes after her aunt," laughed Aunt Ginnie. "We both appreciate good food, don't we? I'll miss having a gourmet cook to teach me."

After they had fetched the hat and some sunscreen from the cottage, they decided to walk the other way, to Uncle Rod's. "He's very eager to see you again," said Aunt Ginnie.

"I wonder why," said her sister dryly. "Rodney and I were never that close, you know."

Uncle Rod was as overbearing as usual, but today it didn't work. "Ruth! My long-lost sister!" He kissed her with a smack, but she stepped back and appraised him calmly.

"How are you, Rodney? You've lost a lot of hair, haven't you? And this must be Karen ... and the children."

Aunt Karen seemed awed by her Eastern glamour. "Don't sit on that chair," she warned, "it's not very clean. Christie, go inside and get your Aunt Ruth a cushion."

Uncle Rod's family came back for dinner and Patricia's mother entertained everyone with witty stories about CBC personalities. She never mentioned Patricia's father and no one asked about him.

"Time for bed," said Aunt Ginnie at ten. "Will you be all right in La Petite by yourself, Patricia?"

"I'll be out soon, darling," promised her mother. All the adults seemed to want to discuss something private.

Patricia tried to fall asleep before her mother came. She knew they had to talk about her father sometime, but she wanted to delay it as long as possible. She tossed in the narrow cot and missed Kelly. She decided to go out to her cousin's window.

Slipping a sweater over her nightgown, Patricia crept up the dark driveway. "Kelly!" she hissed outside the bedroom. There was no answer. Kelly must have fallen asleep and Patricia didn't want to call any louder.

Standing outside the cottage made her feel as much of an outsider as she had at the beginning of the summer. She wandered around to the front, where the voices came in a low murmur from the verandah. Maybe she would go in and say she couldn't sleep. Then she heard her name and couldn't resist crouching under the steps to listen.

"But she's only twelve!" That was Aunt Ginnie. "She's much too young to make that kind of decision!"

"We've always believed in letting Patricia think for herself," said her mother's cool voice. "You won't remember, but *I* was never allowed to. I'll go out and ask her now."

Patricia dashed back to La Petite and jumped into bed. When her mother came into the cabin she pretended to be sound asleep. She held the blanket over her head as a shield against whatever she was going to be asked to decide.

SHE FOUND OUT the next afternoon. "Let's have a talk, darling," said her mother after lunch. As Patricia followed her to La Petite she remembered Nan and *her* awful talk. Nan had been eager, however; her mother seemed as reluctant as she was.

Patricia sat on one bed and curled her arms around her knees. Her mother sat on the other and the space between them seemed appropriately wide.

"Everything has been settled, darling," she began. In a rush she explained that Patricia could see her father whenever she wanted to. "You realize that, even though it's only a separation at this stage, eventually we'll get a divorce. Johanna wants to marry him. I'm telling you this so you don't get your hopes up. It's final."

"I know," said Patricia flatly. "I always have. They love each other."

Her mother looked at her curiously as if surprised she had thought about things so much. Then she became very serious. "There's a change now, darling, and I came West so I could tell you in person. I'm taking a leave of absence, beginning in October. Another job has come up, with the BBC in London. It's for a year—possibly more—and it's a wonderful opportunity I also think it would be a good idea for me to be away until the gossip has died down."

She stood up and began walking around the room. "Now, the question is, darling, whether you want to come with me. You can, of course. We'll find you a good school and I already have a flat lined up. But your father and Johanna have offered to take you for a year. You could stay at the same school then and still be in Toronto. That would be more stable for you—we want to disrupt you as little as possible." She stopped pacing and looked at her daughter directly. "We're leaving it up to you, whether you want to live with me or your father."

Patricia clutched the bed as if she were going to float off. She had never felt so insubstantial.

"You don't have to decide right this minute, darling. Don't look so desolate! I'll stay here until the end of the month and we can discuss it as often as you want. But then you'll have to make up your mind so we can begin all the arrangements. Do you have any questions?"

"If I—if I did live with Daddy and Johanna, what would happen at the end of the year?"

"We'll see how you feel then. You could stay with them or come back to me—whatever you wished. We both ... love you, but we're rational people, Patricia, and we're going to be sensible about this. You're old enough to make up your own mind."

Patricia recalled her mother saying that when she was eight and was asked to choose between staying in her old school or switching to The Learning Place. She hadn't felt old enough then and she didn't now. They had always left important questions up to her, while the trivial ones— what to wear and what activities to participate in—were controlled by her mother. It would be so much easier the other way around.

When she had changed schools she had decided what she guessed her mother wanted. Now it was hard to tell. She yearned for her mother to say that of course she should stay with her. But if she wouldn't say it, she must not want it.

"Here's a letter from your father," her mother continued. "Read what he has to say and that may help you decide. I'll leave you alone for a while, darling.

I suppose this must be a bit of a shock." Patting Patricia's shoulder awkwardly she left the cabin.

"Dear Patricia," her father had typed on his word processor. "Naturally Johanna and I would like to have you live with us this year. It's up to you to make the choice, however, and we don't want to pressure you in any way …" The letter continued in the same apologetic way.

Patricia sighed. Neither of her parents was going to come right out and say they wanted her.

She tried to think it out as reasonably as they suggested. In many ways she would be happier with her father, since she had always felt closer to him. But there was Johanna. Wouldn't she be in the way, just when the two of them were finally able to be together? And she had never particularly cared for her life in Toronto. A new one in a new country though, would be scary.

She knew she couldn't truly decide. As usual, she didn't know what she wanted. She would just have to pretend to make a choice. It was a question of whom she would bother the least—probably Daddy. Her mother would feel much less encumbered in her new job without a daughter to worry about.

"I'll live with Daddy and Johanna," Patricia told her mother that night. "He said they didn't mind."

"Of course they don't *mind*, darling! But are you sure you're ready to decide right now?"

Patricia nodded, trying to gauge her mother's reaction. But all she did was turn her back as she pulled off her clothes and got into her nightgown. She didn't speak again until she turned out the light, and then her voice was chilly.

"It's a very sensible decision, darling, and I'm proud of you for making it yourself. Tomorrow we can phone your father from the store and tell him."

They lay in the darkness and listened to the rustle of the aspen leaves outside.

"I've never liked this cabin," complained Patricia's mother after a few minutes. "It's so small and suffocating."

Patricia didn't answer; she was trying her best not to let her mother hear her cry.

17

*W*hen Patricia told Kelly, her cousin agreed with her decision. "Of course, I don't know your father, but you wouldn't want to leave Canada, would you? England's awfully far away."

Patricia was surprised; she would never have guessed that Kelly would express caution about anything. Perhaps being so contentedly rooted in her family made her a bit complacent.

"It's not because I would mind going to England," she explained, realizing that was true. After all, she had come here from across the country—and had travelled to an even farther place through the watch—and she had survived both.

Kelly clutched Patricia's arm possessively. "I wish you didn't have to go at all! I wish you could live with *us*! I asked Mum, but she said we couldn't interfere."

For the next few days Aunt Ginnie looked grim, as if she wanted to say something to her older sister but didn't dare. "It's not right," Patricia heard her whisper to Aunt Karen. "Girls belong with their mothers."

"But if Patricia chose her father ..."

I didn't choose anyone, thought Patricia listlessly. They forced me to make a decision, that's all.

In a way, it was a relief to have it all out in the open. Patricia's mother chatted easily about London and her husband and sometimes even Johanna's name was mentioned, establishing her as a fact.

Her mother politely took part in the swimming and picnicking and once paddled the *Loon* with a bored efficiency. Each evening she hunched over one of the old puzzles Trevor had set up on the verandah. Watching her gave Patricia a glimpse of Ruth.

But her mother also seemed restless. She drove into town every day to pick up the Toronto newspaper, and once she even complained because there was no TV in the cottage.

"I really shouldn't be staying away this long," she confided to Patricia. "There are so many things I have to wind up before I go."

Patricia hated it every time she mentioned leaving. She never once expressed regret that her daughter wasn't going with her.

On the phone Patricia's father had told her shyly how delighted they were that she would be living with them. That made her feel a bit better. But he had sold his share of the house to Patricia's mother and bought a townhouse with Johanna. The thought of moving was unsettling.

"What will happen to our—to your—house?" she asked her mother.

"I'll rent it … a couple at work are interested in it. But it's still your house too, darling. Don't forget that."

It didn't seem so anymore.

SUNDAY WAS THE ANNUAL Sports Day at the lake. In the morning the Grants watched the last sailboat race of the season from the Donaldsons' deck.

"*Next* year can we get a sailboat?" Kelly asked her father.

"Probably. I hate to say yes when you were so disappointed this year. But I think I could say almost, absolutely, positively—"

"Hurray!" Kelly wrapped him in a vigorous hug.

"Patricia can come back and crew with me, can't you?" Next summer was much too far away for Patricia to imagine. Next month alone was going to be agony to get through.

All afternoon there were events at the Main Beach. Children and dogs thronged the wide pier as someone with a megaphone announced each competition. The people who ran the store sold pop and ice cream from a cooler and several families brought picnics.

Patricia ran in a three-legged race with Christie. It was hard enough to run with one leg anchored to her cousin's, but the race took place in the water, which made it even more difficult. Then she squashed between her cousins in the *Loon* as four of them formed a team in the canoe race. "*Pull ... pull ... pull!*" ordered Kelly, yelling so loud that she lost her voice. There were different kinds of swimming races, a Tug of War and a watermelon-eating contest, but the only member of the family who won a ribbon was Peggy, in the Dog Paddle. In the midst of it all, Patricia tried her best to enjoy herself, to forget that her new life was about to begin.

"Your swimming has really improved, darling," Patricia's mother told her when she came in from the water to rest. "Don't you find the water awfully weedy though? I don't remember the lake being this full of them."

"It wasn't. It used to be much cleaner and colder," said Patricia without thinking. "Uncle Rod told me that," she added hastily.

"I wonder how long this is going to last," her mother complained. She was causing quite a stir; people who knew her from TV stared curiously and others came up and asked if she remembered them from earlier summers.

Aunt Ginnie was helping an old woman arrange her lawn chair on the sand. "This is Mrs. Thorpe," she told Patricia. "A friend of Nan's."

Patricia shook the woman's hand curiously. She must be Barbara and Winnie and Paul's mother; some of the Other Enders were their children. She wondered if Mrs. Thorpe was still a light sleeper.

THE DAY AFTER Sports Day there was a terrific storm. They all sat on the lawn before dinner and watched it approach. On their side of the lake it was still sunny and still. On the other side, dark grey clouds collected and lightning flickered. The boom of thunder became louder as the water darkened and rippled towards them.

"Get ready to pick up a chair and run!" laughed Aunt Ginnie. In a few minutes the sun disappeared, trees began swaying and huge drops of cold rain fell.

"Just in time!" panted Kelly, slamming the screen door after the last person had scuttled inside.

Rain poured down as if someone had turned on a tap. "Just what the farmers need," said Uncle Doug. "It's been such a dry summer."

Patricia jumped at the sound of a deafening peal of thunder. She stood at the window with the rest of the family and watched in awe as lightning split the huge sky.

"Quite a spectacle, isn't it, Patricia?" said her uncle. "There's nothing like a prairie thunderstorm for fireworks."

Patricia nodded, but the violence of the thunder made her jump every time. She was relieved when the storm finally settled into a steady drumming of rain on the roof.

Trevor put out Snakes and Ladders, Maggie's favourite game, on the verandah floor. They played it enough to satisfy her, and then went on to Clue. After dinner they joined the adults in a game of Trivial Pursuit in the living room. The fire crackled cheerfully as they took a break for second helpings of saskatoon pie.

Patricia spooned up the purple juice greedily. She and her cousins had spent all morning picking the dusty blue berries and the delicious result was worth it.

They finished the game. Patricia and her mother won, but it was her mother, not she, who knew all the answers.

Aunt Ginnie was observing her sister thoughtfully. Then she took down the photograph from the mantel. "Do you remember this, Ruth? How funny we all looked!"

Patricia's mother took the picture and glanced at it briefly. "No, I don't," she said. "Why were we dressed like that?"

"It was a costume party. In those days, people at the lake got together more often, not just once a summer for Sports Day. But surely you remember—you were about Patricia's age. Even I can remember dressing up in Gordon's clothes and feeling so important because I was allowed to go. But I ate too much and got sick. And wasn't that the night poor Mama lost her watch? She's often told me how she searched for days—"

"I don't remember it," interrupted Patricia's mother crisply. She handed the picture back.

Aunt Ginnie looked hurt and there was an awkward silence. Then her sister said abruptly, "I've decided to change my plans. Since Patricia has already chosen what she wants to do, there's no need for us to stay here another week. Mother is insisting that we visit her in Calgary. We could get a connecting flight and just go for a day. We'll leave tomorrow. Can you drive us into the city in the afternoon, Doug?"

"Tomorrow! But you can't!"

Everyone protested, but Patricia's mother was firm. "Can you, Doug?" she kept asking and he finally had to consent.

"And now, if you'll all excuse me"—she smiled charmingly at them—"I have a headache. I think I'll go to bed."

After she left, Patricia's cousins surrounded her. "Mum, she can't go!" said Kelly, almost in tears. "It's not fair, she was supposed to stay until the end of the summer."

Maggie flung her long arms around Patricia's neck. "Don't leave, Patty!" she begged.

"There's nothing I can do," Aunt Ginnie told them. She pressed her lips together tightly. "It's up to her mother. Patricia, dear, you know we want you to come back next summer, don't you? I'm sure your father will let you."

Uncle Doug ruffled her hair and Peggy licked her hand. Patricia tried to smile at them all. "I think I'll go to bed, too," she said softly.

All the way out to La Petite she shook with fury, not noticing that she'd forgotten her jacket and was getting soaked. She kicked open the door and stomped in.

Her mother, sitting in bed with a book, looked up and frowned. "Don't bang it, darling."

Patricia marched over to the bed. Her anger rushed out of her like the torrent of rain that had descended earlier. Its power didn't surprise her as much as it had with Nan.

"How can you decide we have to leave so suddenly?" she shouted. "Why didn't you ever tell me about your summers at the lake? Why do you have to keep pretending you don't remember anything and hurt Aunt Ginnie's feelings? *I* don't want to leave! And Aunt Ginnie said I could come back. I wish I lived with them all the time! At least they *want* me, n-not like you ..." She stopped to get her breath.

Patricia's mother looked astonished. "Darling ..." she began.

"Don't *call* me that!" raged Patricia. "I hate it! I always have! You say darling because you don't know me—because you don't c-care about me and you don't want me to live with you." Then all she could do was to gulp down ugly sobs.

"Patricia," whispered her mother. Tears welled up in her beautiful eyes—eyes that looked young without makeup. Then she was weeping, too. Patricia was so shocked, her own tears subsided. She had never seen her mother cry.

Except once, on a miserable night after she had been unfairly scolded for raiding the camp. That sobbing girl and this woman were the same person. The Ruth in the past hadn't vanished at all. She was inside this person who wailed like a child, saying in a beseeching voice between gulps, "Oh, Patricia, Patricia ..."

"Mum." Patricia sat down weakly on her mother's bed. "I'm sorry I didn't mean it."

"No, dar—Patricia. *I'm* sorry You're right to be angry with me." Ruth blew her nose and handed a kleenex to Patricia. "But you're wrong, too. I do want you. I do care about you. I was longing for you to say you'd come with me, but it didn't seem fair to ask. And when you made your decision, I thought you didn't want *me*. Oh, Patricia, will you come to London? If you don't, I'll miss you so much I don't think I could bear it?"

Patricia's chest expanded with lightness. "Do you—do you really want me?"

"Of course I want you! You're my daughter. I love you. I guess I haven't let you know that enough. I've never known how to be a good mother, Patricia, but can we be friends?"

Patricia gazed at Ruth with brimming eyes. She had wanted so much to be friends with her in the past. She had wanted so much to comfort her. Now she could.

She nodded so hard her tears scattered onto the bed. "Okay. And I *will* come with you. Daddy won't mind. They need to be by themselves right now, anyhow. And I never did like The Learning Place. I think I'm too ordinary for it."

"Ordinary!" Ruth pulled her daughter onto her lap. "You're the most special person in the world."

After more tears and more hugs, they began to talk about London.

18

*T*hen Patricia decided to show Ruth the watch. They had three days left at the lake. Ruth had compromised, and Patricia didn't mind so much now about leaving early. They were going to spend the weekend with Nan in Calgary, and it was this which made up Patricia's mind. She finally had to do something about the watch. Ruth could help her decide what.

She knew she could never tell her everything. Not about how she had visited the past and watched her then. No one would believe that.

She was going to have to confess that she'd concealed the watch all summer. It filled her with guilt again, but she reminded herself that Ruth was just as much to blame.

The next afternoon the family decided to drive into town. "Can we stay here?" Patricia asked her mother. "There's something I have to show you."

Ruth waited in the rocking chair while Patricia trudged down the attic stairs, the watch a cold handful of metal in her palm.

"Here?" She poured the watch and chain into Ruth's lap.

Her mother gasped. "Where on earth did you get this, Patricia?"

"I—I found it in La Petite in July. It was under the floorboards," she continued, as if Ruth didn't know. "Uncle Doug had ripped up the old linoleum. I know I should have shown it to someone, but I—I kind of liked it … so I kept it in the attic. But it must be the watch Nan lost, so I'd better give it back. Do you think she'll be angry?"

Ruth didn't speak for a moment. She ran her fingers up and down the chain in wonder. "I can't say—I just can't say how glad I am that you found this, Patricia," she murmured finally. "I think I'd better tell you something about it and then you won't worry about Nan."

Patricia waited, her former awe of her mother returning. Now she was going to admit how she'd deliberately kept the watch from Nan.

"When I was your age," her mother began, her voice shaky, "I had a very bad summer here. I felt picked on and alienated from everyone in the family—especially from my mother. She tried to force me to be something I wasn't—a 'nice young lady' who would make a good marriage. She wouldn't accept me as I was." Ruth paused and looked into Patricia's eyes. "I guess I've done the same with you … not seen who you really are." She looked down for a minute, then went on. "Anyway, the night of that costume party—which I do remember in every detail—" she added sheepishly, "I found the watch on the road soon after Mother had lost it. La Petite had just been built the summer before and the floor was only bare boards. I pried one up and hid the watch under it. It was a shameful thing to do, and I've always felt terribly guilty about it. For that and other reasons my relationship with Mother got worse and worse. I decided to leave home as soon as I could. When I won a scholarship to the University of Toronto they couldn't stop me, though Father certainly tried."

"Why didn't you give the watch back?" Patricia couldn't help asking.

"I meant to. I meant to keep it hidden for just a few days. It gave me a feeling of power over Mother— I wanted to make her suffer. And then I was going to return it in triumph and she'd be so grateful she'd never yell at me again," said Ruth dryly. Her face flushed. "But I kept putting it off. I was very bitter in those days. In many ways I had a right to be—but not that much. Then a friend from school asked me to stay with her on another lake. All the two weeks I was away I felt terrible and I swore I'd return the watch the minute I got back. But when I returned—oh, Patricia!—Father had put down linoleum. The watch was sealed underneath and I couldn't—I just *couldn't*—ask them to pull up the floor. Then I would have had to confess and be even more in their black books. It was cowardly and I've never forgiven myself for it."

Patricia could see how difficult it would have been to tell. But she was relieved that Ruth hadn't meant to keep the watch from her mother forever.

"We can give it to her now," she said softly.

"Yes, we can!" agreed Ruth. "She'll be so excited! Did you know it belonged to her first fiancé? She cared for it a great deal."

"When Nan was here she said some things that were quite … awful," said Patricia slowly, peering at her mother to see her reaction. "She might be really mad I kept the watch all this time."

"I kept it from her much longer! Yes, Mother can be fierce. She's had a disappointing life in many ways and sometimes her anger about it erupts. But I guess at some point we have to forgive our parents." She smiled ruefully at her daughter. "Even if they don't deserve it. Mother and I have become so used to not getting along that it's become a bad habit. But maybe this will change things. Maybe now she'll forgive *me*. It's not necessary to say where the watch has been all these years, as long as we give it back. We'll tell your Nan—we'll tell everyone—you've just found the watch under a rock or something. It will be our own guilty secret, all right?"

Patricia grinned with relief. "All right." She recalled Nan suggesting that she and Patricia begin again. Perhaps all three of them could make a fresh start. Sometimes it might be best to forget the past. Or at least accept it, and then keep on going.

And she would never completely forget the special secret feeling of being in that time. She picked up the watch and swung it back and forth. "It doesn't work," she said wistfully. "I keep trying to wind it, but it's broken."

Ruth laughed. "You'd hardly expect it to work after lying under a floor for thirty-five years! Mother won't care, she'll be so overjoyed to have it at all. Did you read the inscription?" They bent over the watch together.

"Here you are!" Kelly and Trevor and Maggie burst through the door. "We bought you some comics, Patricia," said Kelly. "Why don't we go to the fort? Then we can go swimming and try out Bruce's new snorkel and then we'll fix the raft. You still have a few days. Let's not waste them!"

"Go on," smiled Ruth. "I'll wait for Ginnie and show her the watch."

AFTER ALL THE RAIN the path was so muddy that Patricia had to straddle it on the hilly parts, gripping the bank on each side with her toes to keep from slipping.

She descended the steps to the beach, pulled the canoe into the water and steered it into the path of the setting sun. The water broke in little waves against the sides. Resting the paddle, she let the boat drift and waited to hear the loon. Above her, the trees were black shadows against the dim sky. Her family's voices drifted down from the cottage; they were all inside, but Patricia had come out alone to say goodbye to the lake.

She didn't want to leave tomorrow. The thought of going to England was exciting but scary. Even though she and Ruth were now friends, it would take a while to get used to each other's real selves.

And Ruth was still her mother. Yesterday Patricia had seethed with irritation after hearing all morning about the countless fussy preparations for their trip. Then she remembered how Ruth needed to feel in control. She surprised herself by saying to her mother in a teasing voice, "Relax, Mum. We'll get to London somehow, even if everything isn't done perfectly."

Patricia wondered where she would be next summer. She might come here again ... or she might not. Nothing was certain but the calm water around her and the tremulous bird call she finally heard.

Then she saw the loon for the first time. It glided ahead of her, peering around warily with its dark, straight-beaked head, its broad back half-submerged. It sank into the water and disappeared.

For an instant Patricia didn't know what time she was in. The lake and the loon's cry were out of time. They had been there before the Indians came, part of one endless summer that extended infinitely into the past and the future.

Then time settled into the present and Patricia paddled towards the shore.

ACKNOWLEDGEMENTS

Many thanks to Philippa Pearce and Oxford University Press for permission to use the lines from *Tom's Midnight Garden* (1958); and to my editor, David Kilgour, who helped me discover what I really meant.

ALSO IN THE GUESTS OF WAR TRILOGY!

WINNER OF THE MR. CHRISTIE BOOK AWARD, THE GEOFFREY BILSON AWARD FOR HISTORICAL FICTION FOR YOUNG PEOPLE, AND THE CANADIAN LIBRARY ASSOCIATION'S BOOK OF THE YEAR FOR CHILDREN

It is the summer of 1940, and all of England fears an invasion by Hitler's army. Still, ten-year-old Norah Stoakes is shocked when her parents decide to send her and her younger brother, Gavin, to Canada as war guests. Travelling across the ocean is an adventure, but Norah's new life in Canada is a bigger challenge that she ever expected. Until, that is, Norah discovers a surprising responsibility that helps her accept her new country and her new home.

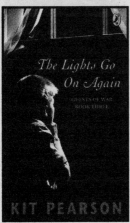

WINNER OF THE IODE VIOLET DOWNEY AWARD AND THE GEOFFREY BILSON AWARD FOR HISTORICAL FICTION FOR YOUNG PEOPLE

It has been five years since Norah and Gavin arrived in Canada, and how that the war is ending, they will soon be going back to England. Norah is eager to see her parents again, but ten-year-old Gavin barely remembers them. He doesn't want to leave his Canadian family, his two best friends, and his dog. Then something happens that forces Gavin to make the most difficult decision of his life.

"A first rate trilogy..."
—*The Globe and Mail*

 www.kitpearson.ca